Bella Broomstick

Bella Broomstick

LOU KUENZLER

ILLUSTRATED BY
KYAN CHENG

SCHOLASTIC

Scholastic Children's Books
An imprint of Scholastic Ltd
Euston House, 24 Eversholt Street, London, NW1 1DB, UK
Registered office: Westfield Road, Southam, Warwickshire, CV47 0RA
SCHOLASTIC and associated logos are trademarks and/or
registered trademarks of Scholastic Inc.

First published in the UK by Scholastic Ltd, 2015

Text copyright © Lou Kuenzler, 2016
Front cover copyright © Nicola Slater, 2016
Illustration copyright © Kyan Cheng, 2016

The right of Lou Kuenzler and Kyan Cheng to be identified as the author and
illustrator of this work has been asserted by them.

ISBN 978 1407 15795 5

A CIP catalogue record for this book
is available from the British Library.

Printed by CPI Group (UK) Ltd, Croydon, CR0 4YY
Papers used by Scholastic Children's Books are made
from wood grown in sustainable forests.

1 3 5 7 9 10 8 6 4 2

www.scholastic.co.uk

To my family. You are magic!

– LK

I'm drawing this with a stick and swamp mud!

Chapter One

I am a hopeless witch.

Everybody says so.

Especially Aunt Hemlock. She woke me up at dawn this morning just to tell me how hopeless I am.

"Belladonna Broomstick, you are the most hopeless young witch in the whole of the Magic Realm!" she said, poking me with her long fingernails as the seven warts on the end of her nose wobbled like fat green frogs.

I don't have any warts on my nose. Perhaps that's why I'm such a hopeless witch?

No nose hair

No warts

Nose hair

Wonderful warts

Frown

Smile

Ferret smell

ME

NORMAL WITCH

If I could grow just one teeny-tiny wart, I might learn to be good at magic.

I yawned and peeped at my reflection in Aunt Hemlock's magic mirror.

"Aha!" cackled the mirror. "If it's not

Belladonna Broomstick. Just look at your big brown eyes and chocolate curls. Not a wart in sight. Pathetic. What a hopeless young witch!"

"Actually, Bella, I think you're very pretty," whispered a spider that swung down from the roof of the cave.

"Thank you," I blushed, understanding every word he'd said. Speaking animal languages is the only thing I am any good at.

Belladonna Broomstick's Magic Skills
Wand Work: HOPELESS
Spells: HOPELESS
Potions: HOPELESS
Talking to Animals: EXCELLENT!!

YIPPEE!

"Quiet!" Aunt Hemlock grabbed the poor little spider by seven of his eight long legs

3

and dunked him in her lumpy porridge.

"Let him go!" I cried.

As if by magic (which it probably was), Aunt Hemlock's creepy chameleon, Wane, appeared on the kitchen shelf. Wane gives me the shivers. I never know what colour he is going to be or where he will appear next. He's always spying on me and telling tales to Aunt Hemlock. Right now he was disguising himself behind a jar of frogspawn.

"Yum! Is that spider for me, mistress?" he slurped, sticking out his long purple tongue.

"Certainly not!" Aunt Hemlock dangled the spider above her open mouth. "This one is mine."

"Stop!" I begged, but Aunt Hemlock swallowed the poor thing whole. "How horrible!" I shuddered.

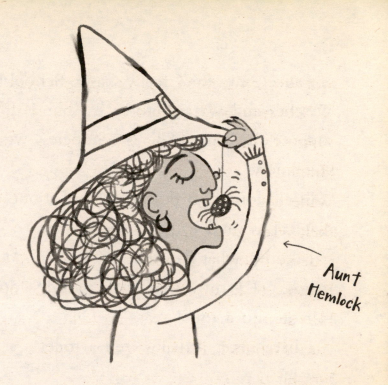

Aunt Hemlock

"And very unfair not to share," sulked Wane, turning piglet-pink in a huff.

Aunt Hemlock ignored us both and picked her teeth with a chicken bone.

"You're looking marvellously magical today, if I may say so, mistress," said the mirror, sucking up to her as usual.

"At least one of us is looking magical," sighed Aunt Hemlock. "Belladonna has her entrance exam for Creepy Castle School for Witches and Wizards today … but I don't suppose she'll pass. She is a hopeless witch, you know."

"Belladonna Broomstick is about as magical as mud," agreed the mirror.

I know what I'd do if I was good at magic… I'd turn that vain, goody-goody mirror into a toilet seat.

I have never actually seen a toilet seat in real life.

Stinging nettles (ouch!)

But I know what they look like because I've seen a picture in the Sellwell Department Store Catalogue — a wonderful, shiny book I found blowing about on the moors one day. I have no idea where it came from ...

perhaps the Person World? Most witches and wizards my age say there is no such place. But I keep the catalogue hidden under my bed and peep at the washing machines and fridges every night. Even if it is only a fairy tale, it can't hurt to dream…

"Hold on!" said Wane. "Hasn't Belladonna already taken the exam for Creepy Castle…?" He gave a nasty little smile. I began to imagine all the things I'd like to turn him into, too.

SELLWELL DEPARTMENT STORE CATALOGUE
Lizard-shaped salt shaker
(Page 183)

"Belladonna has taken the examination *twice* before," sighed Aunt Hemlock.

I knew what was coming next…

"And she has *failed* it twice too!"

"Third time lucky?" I said, crossing my fingers behind my back.

"How hilarious!" The mirror laughed so hard it nearly fell off the wall.

"Not a hope, Belladonna!" wheezed Wane. His dry, lizardy voice sounded as if he'd swallowed a bucket of sand. "You are your parents' daughter, after all…"

"Don't you dare be rude about my parents," I said loudly in my best lizard language, so that even stupid Wane could understand me.

Everyone says my mum and dad were no good at magic. When I was a baby, they turned themselves into white mice to make me laugh. It wasn't a very good

9

idea – not in the Magic Realm with so many witches' cats about (not to mention big, greedy lizards!). All that was ever found were two pink tails…

That's why I live with Aunt Hemlock.

"Mum and Dad might not have been very good at magic, but at least they were kind," I said.

"Kind?" Wane's big round eyes nearly popped right out of his head. "Fat lot of good that did them!"

"You horrible, leather-headed bully!" I picked up a wooden spoon and waved it like an ogre's cudgel. Wane shot behind a cactus and turned prickly and green.

"Goodie," cackled the mirror. "A fight!"

Aunt Hemlock stepped between us. "This exam had better be third time lucky, Belladonna Broomstick, or I'll dip you in porridge and gobble you up like that spider." She snatched another one off the wall and swallowed it whole, just to make her point. "If you fail this time, you won't get another chance."

I wish I had a proper pen to doodle with. This one is my favourite!

SELLWELL DEPARTMENT STORE CATALOGUE
Flamingo pen
(Page 118)

Chapter Two

The exam hall at Creepy Castle was in the deepest, darkest, dampest dungeon in the whole school.

My desk was at the very back, right next to Nightshade Newtbreath (worst luck).

"Hee hee," giggled Nightshade, showing off her perfectly chipped green teeth and sticking her (extremely) warty nose in the air. "I bet you won't even be able to answer the first question, Belladonna

Broomstick … or should I say, Belladonna Broom*thick*?"

"Very funny!" I groaned. From the way Nightshade was laughing you'd think I'd never heard her silly Broomthick joke before. Nightshade is in my class at the Toadstool Spell Group, where witches and wizards go before we're old enough for Creepy Castle. I have been there a long time, because I had to repeat the year – twice. Nightshade never lets me forget it.

"Look!" she giggled, pointing at Dr Rattlebone, the ancient skeleton teacher who was overseeing the test. "You'll be as old as him before you pass this exam."

"I'm not that old! Dr Rattlebone has been dead for nearly a thousand years," I said. "I'm only just in double figures."

Dr Rattlebone rapped his bony fingers on the desk. "Silence, please," he rattled. "You may turn over your parchments and begin."

There was a swishing sound like a hundred bat wings. I looked up at the roof of the dungeon, but the school bats were sleeping. I realized it wasn't wings I could hear – it was the sound of a hundred parchments fluttering over ready for the exam to begin. Every other young witch and wizard in the room had done this simply by waving their wands at the page.

I scrabbled in my bag. My wand was a horrible old thing, with a terrible temper like an angry rat. "Ouch!" I yelped as a sharp splinter jabbed me in the finger.

I waved the wand at the page three times. (If you do anything three times in magic, there's a chance it might work.) Nothing happened.

"Having a problem, Belladonna?" hissed Nightshade.

"No!" I waved my wand again. One, two, three times...

POOF! A great orangey-red flame shot on to the desk.

"Help! Fire!" screamed Nightshade.

"Belladonna has set her test paper alight."

It wasn't only the paper – the big green bow in Nightshade's hair was looking a little smoky, too.

I leapt to my feet, knocking over my chair, as everyone else in the room gasped.

"Spinning spiders, I didn't mean that to happen!" I cried, trying to put out the flames with my wand. Unfortunately, that only made things worse. The burning paper spun in the air like a firework.

"I've never seen anything like this in over nine hundred years of teaching," said

Dr Rattlebone, putting out the flames with his wand. "A very disappointing start, Belladonna." He shook his skull so hard that it fell off his neck and rolled past my feet.

"Now look what you've done!" Nightshade leapt up to pass Dr Rattlebone back his head. "I don't think Belladonna ought to be in the same exam room as the rest of us," she whined. "She is far too dangerous, sir."

MY WORST MAGIC MISTAKES EVER

Vanishing Spell - only my bottom half disappeared but it was missing for a whole week.

Lizard Levitation - I dropped Wane in mid-air

Turn Yourself Into A Toad Spell - unfortunately, I waved my wand at Aunt Hemlock by mistake.

"Have a go at the first spell," sighed Dr Rattlebone, balancing his skull back on his bony neck. "If you haven't blown up the dungeon by then, I might let you carry on."

"Thank you," I whispered, bending over the fresh parchment that had magically appeared on my desk.

TASK ONE: Using your wand, turn your shoelace into a worm.

I felt a leap of hope. I'd read up on the Shoelace Hex last night. I looked down and saw the floor crawling with fat pink worms that the other students had already made.

Swish! Swish! Swish! I waved my lumpy old wand up and down three times in a *wriggly-squiggly* worm movement. It was no good. My long brown shoelace was still trailing from my boot in a half-tied knot.

I was just getting ready to try again when a scream from Nightshade made me jump.

"Belladonna, look what you've done!" she wailed. Curling its way out of her shoe was a giant snake!

"Hopeless!" groaned Dr Rattlebone. "Your wand movements were far too big, Belladonna."

I crouched down and hissed politely to the snake. "Welcome, friend!" He was a lot more exciting than a wiggly worm.

"Do something!" screamed Nightshade as the slippery snake slithered around her ankle.

Kaboom! With one wave of his spindly arm, Dr Rattlebone exploded the snake with his wand.

"Poor thing!" I gasped (though I suppose it was only a shoelace really).

"That does it." Dr Rattlebone's bony fingers grabbed my collar and he marched me towards the door. "You have failed the examination!"

Everyone (even Nightshade) was deathly quiet now. My heart was pounding like a frog on a chopping board. "Please, sir, give me one last chance," I begged.

But Dr Rattlebone shook his head so hard it toppled off his neck again.

"You have had your last chance, Belladonna Broomstick!" His skull rattled as it bounced across the floor. "You will never be a student at Creepy Castle School for Witches and Wizards!"

Chapter Three

"Failed?" Aunt Hemlock tore the note from Dr Rattlebone out of my hand.

STUDENT NAME:

Belladonna Broomstick

Score: 0/100

Test Result: FAIL

Never come back! Ever!

Signed: D. Rattlebone (Deceased)

ZAP! She waved her wand and the parchment ripped into a thousand tiny pieces. *ZING!* The jagged shreds of paper turned into a swarm of angry wasps.

Buzzzzzzzzzzzzzzzzzzzzzzzzz.

No, not wasps – giant hornets! Each one had a stinger as long as a pin.

"Blistering bugs!" I ducked under the table, sure that the stripy swarm would attack me. But they shot straight out of the cave door. I didn't blame them. The mood Aunt Hemlock was in, she would probably turn them into a spicy hornet curry – stings and all.

"What am I going to do with you?" she thundered as purple steam poured from her ears. "What use is a witch who cannot do the simplest magic?"

"I could learn," I stammered.

"*Where?*" Aunt Hemlock's green warts were wobbling like nettle jelly. "Where can you learn to be a proper witch now that you have failed to get a place at Creepy Castle?"

"I – I don't know," I sighed. She had a point. Creepy Castle is the only school this side of the Magic Mountains.

"Perhaps I could stay at home and practise my animal languages?" I said. I can already make myself understood with nearly all the common creatures in the Magic Realm.

Lizard Lisp: Good (only way to find out what Wane is up to next).

Spider Speak: Good (plenty of practice in the cave).

Bat Shriek, Snake Spiel and Owl Hoot: Not bad.

Hornet Hum, Frog Croak and Toad Talk: Improving.

****Cat Chat: Best of all.
(My favourite language)****

"Talking to animals? What's the point in that?" snarled Aunt Hemlock. "The only thing dumb creatures are any good for is boiling up in potions and spells."

"Charming!" gulped Wane as he scuttled well away from the bubbling cauldron.

"Belladonna could always volunteer at the potions laboratory," laughed the magic mirror. "The magicians could practise on her until they get their mixtures just right."

"That is not a bad idea." Aunt Hemlock's

green eyes sparkled. "Seeing as you like animals so much, Belladonna, you could be a sort of guinea pig for the laboratory." She raised her wand.

POOF!

The air fizzled out of me like a popped balloon and I shrunk to the ground.

"Eek! What am I doing down here?" I peered out from under a long fringe of shaggy orange hair. All I could think about was how much I wanted to eat a carrot … or maybe a nice fat sunflower seed and a hunk of lettuce.

I stared up at the mirror and squeaked. Aunt Hemlock had turned me into a guinea pig!

"Hilarious!" said Wane, laughing until he was tartan all over. "But I've got a better idea."

Aunt Hemlock sighed and waved her wand. "Let's hear it, then."

PING!

I turned back into a girl. I shook my arms and counted my fingers. Ten. I wriggled my toes. They were all there too. Phew! Fingers and toes are always getting left behind after a spell.

Everything was back to normal … except, I still would have given anything to eat a nice juicy carrot.

"Belladonna should get a job with the trolls in the cauldron factory," sniggered Wane.

"Belladonna *is* about as stupid as a troll!" Aunt Hemlock smiled.

"I wouldn't mind," I said. It's hard work

at the factory, melting iron inside a roaring volcano. But my friend Gawpaw is a troll. He says that once the shift is over, they dance to tin flutes and cook stew in an iron pot as big as a bathtub – not that I've ever actually seen a bathtub except in the Sellwell Department Store Catalogue (page 73). Aunt Hemlock makes me wash in the swamp.

"Trolls aren't stupid," I said. "Gawpaw knows—"

"Enough!" Aunt Hemlock raised her hand. "No niece of mine, no matter how hopeless, is going to work amongst those smelly creatures."

That was pretty funny, coming from Aunt Hemlock. She stinks of rotten eggs, garlic and cheesy feet … except on wash night, when she smells of swamp mud.

"If you cannot learn to be a proper young witch, then there is only one place for you," said Aunt Hemlock with an evil grin.

"No! Not…" The mirror gasped and shivered on the slimy green wall.

"Surely you don't mean…?" Wane peeped out at Aunt Hemlock from behind his two-toed hands. "Is that wise, mistress?"

"Where are you going to send me?" I asked. Surely whatever she was planning couldn't be worse than working inside a roaring volcano or being experimented on in a potions lab?

"It's perfect! I can't believe I didn't think of it sooner." Aunt Hemlock threw back her head and laughed. "Belladonna Broomstick, I am going to send you to live in the Person World."

"The Person World?" I felt as if a thousand fawns were leaping inside my tummy. "You mean, where the human beings live?"

Nightshade Newtbreath says only babies believe in the Person World. Witches and wizards tell their children about it to scare them and make them be good – there are strange stories about the Wart Stealer, toothbrushes and the No-More-Bogey Man. But ever since I found the Sellwell Department Store Catalogue, I knew it was real!

"The Person World will suit you perfectly,"

cackled Aunt Hemlock. "There is no magic at all, and Persons are so stupid, you should fit right in. After all, Belladonna Broomstick, you are—"

"A hopeless witch," I beamed. For once I didn't mind a bit. I was off to the Person World — the land of toilet seats and fluffy slippers. That was magic enough for me.

Chapter Four

I clung to Aunt Hemlock's waist as we shot through the darkness on her broomstick. "Hold tight," she barked. "We're coming to the edge of the Magic Realm."

"I'm holding as tight as I can," I gulped as my pointy witch's hat blew away in the wind.

"Don't worry. You won't be needing that again," she laughed.

Bam! Something cold and slimy hit me in the face. "Ouch! What was that?" I cried.

"The Curtain of Invisibility," hissed Aunt Hemlock. "It is drawn around the Magic Mountains to keep the witches and wizards hidden from the Person World."

How could something invisible hurt so much? It was like being slapped in the mouth by a big wet fish. I struggled to keep my balance, but toppled off the broom and began to tumble through the dark sky.

Just in time, I grabbed hold of the bristles on the back of the broom. "That was a close one!" I cried as I dangled in mid-air.

"You'll just have to stay like that. I'm not stopping," snapped Aunt Hemlock.

My arm felt as if it was going to be wrenched from its socket, but at least I couldn't smell Aunt Hemlock's stinky old cloak down here. "Are we nearly there yet?"

"I wouldn't be in such a hurry if I was

you," laughed Wane. He was riding in front of Aunt Hemlock like a dragon on the prow of a ship. "Persons eat witches for their tea, you know!"

"Scuttling scorpions!" I gasped. I could see a ring of bright lights glowing in the distance. Were the Persons lighting a fire ready to boil me in a pot? But I thought of the Sellwell catalogue rolled up secretly in the bottom of my travelling sack. Wane didn't know anything. The Person World was good and kind... I was sure of it.

As we flew on, I realized the glow beneath us was just a line of tall lanterns twinkling in the darkness. "How pretty," I whispered.

"They're only street lights," sighed Aunt Hemlock. I scrambled back on to the broom as we swooped over a signpost:

WELCOME TO
MERRYMEET VILLAGE.
Please Drive Carefully.

"Ha! Doesn't say anything about flying though, does it!" she chuckled, looping the loop.

"Help!" I cried, hanging upside down.

"I feel broom-sick!" groaned Wane.

"What a lily-livered pair you are!" whooped Aunt Hemlock as we dive-bombed a village green with a duck pond in the middle and rows of snug little houses all around. She raised her wand and waved it above the rooftops, muttering a strange chant:

Persons round this ring of green,
Let your secret dreams be seen!
Rise foolish thoughts and show the way
To where this hopeless witch will stay.

My heart gave a leap. This was the villiage where I was going to live. "Will your spell really show us my new home?" I asked.

"Precisely. Keep your eyes peeled," Aunt Hemlock cackled. "You'll know what we're looking for when you see it!"

I stared down at the sleeping village with its rows of moonlit cottages. Strange brightly coloured mist rose out of their chimneys and filled the sky.

Aunt Hemlock shook her head. "None of those are the dreams we're after."

We flew on over chestnut trees and narrow winding streets. A burbling river flowed under a humpback bridge, and roses rambled over low stone walls.

It was the prettiest place I had ever seen —
all except for one big dark house, hunched
like a cold grey rock on the far side of the
village green. As we flew closer, I saw high
iron railings covered with sharp barbed wire
that coiled like snakes around the top of
the spikes.

"Cool security!" whistled Wane.

"I do like the bars on the windows.
Gives it such a lovely dungeon feel," Aunt
Hemlock agreed.

My heart plunged like a stone in a well.
This would be just the sort of place Aunt
Hemlock was looking for, I was sure of it.

Suddenly the courtyard was filled with
light. There was a sound of a hundred locks
and bolts being undone as the door swung
open.

"Who's there?" shouted a man as thin as
a wand. "I'll call the police!"

Police? I thought of the giant one-eyed Cyclops Cops who stamp out trouble in the Magic Realm. Would the Person Police be as scary as that?

"Nosy busy-body! I've got a good mind to put a hex on him," thundered Aunt Hemlock as we shot over the roof like a firecracker. My heart soared as we left the grim grey house behind. We weren't stopping there after all.

"Look!" cried Aunt Hemlock, swooping over the spiky fence and hovering above a bird table in the garden next door. "This is the one! I knew my spell would lead the way."

I peered over her shoulder and saw an adorable white cottage with a thatched roof. Out of the chimney came a shining swirl of pink and silver smoke.

"Quick!" Aunt Hemlock whispered. "Where's my snare?" She scrabbled underneath her cloak and pulled out a ragged butterfly net.

"Catch it!" cried Wane as the smoky mist swirled all around us.

"You can't catch smoke in a net," I said, confused.

But Aunt Hemlock hunched forward. "This isn't smoke – it's magic!" She pulled a narrow glass jar from her pocket and plunged it into the net. "Got you!" she grinned, slamming the lid on tight.

Aunt Hemlock held up the jar in a stream of moonlight. The smoke was gone and a pale silvery moth was beating its wings against the glass.

"The poor thing!" I cried. "Let it go!"

"Certainly not." Aunt Hemlock pointed at the pretty white cottage. "The foolish Persons who live here have a dream –

something they have always hoped for. I have caught their hope and turned it into this moth."

She stabbed the lid of the jar with her sharp green fingernails, making two small air holes. "Let's hear what it has to say, shall we?" She raised the jar to her ear. "Idiots…" she laughed. "Fools."

"What?" grinned Wane. "What do the Persons hope for?"

"Yes, tell us," I whispered, looking down at the cosy little cottage and wondering who might live inside. My heart was fluttering as fast as the moth in the jar.

"They hope," said Aunt Hemlock slowly, "for a child."

Chapter Five

"Fizzing ferrets!" I gulped, as Aunt Hemlock landed the broom outside the pretty white cottage. "The Persons who live here want a child?" I watched the fragile hope-moth flutter in the jar. "That's perfect. If they want a child … they might want *me*."

"You!" Aunt Hemlock snorted. "Who'd want you?"

"Even Persons aren't that stupid," sniggered Wane.

"They hope for a child. That's a start at least. But we'll have to use very powerful magic before any Person would agree to take on somebody like you," said Aunt Hemlock, shaking the jar so hard the poor moth turned topsy-turvy.

"More magic. Of course." I sunk down inside my tattered black cloak. "How silly of me." I could smell the sweet scent of the honeysuckle tumbling over the cottage door. It was the prettiest house in the whole village, with its wishing well on the lawn and window boxes full of flowers. In the glow of a lamp hanging in the porch, I could see that the front door was painted sunflower yellow, and a mat on the step said: WELCOME! I should have known it would never be possible for me to live in a pretty little cottage like this. Not without tricking the Persons with a spell.

"Disgusting little place, isn't it?" Aunt Hemlock shuddered. "Sweet as a cupcake. Yuck!"

"Revolting!" Wane stuck out his purple tongue and made a gagging sound.

But they were wrong. I couldn't think of anywhere I'd rather live. "Honeysuckle Cottage", I whispered, reading the name on the door. "If we have to use magic, then let's do it," I fumbled for my wand. "Ouch!" As usual an angry splinter jabbed my finger. "Here goes!" If there was ever a spell I had wanted to get right, it was this one.

I'll just say what I feel, I thought, waving my wand in the air.

"Roof of straw and yellow front door
Be my home for ever more..."

"What are you doing?" cried Aunt Hemlock. She spread her arms like a swooping bat and dived in front of me. "You're not allowed to do magic in the Person World – not without an examination certificate." She waved her own wand under my nose. "If you had been offered a place at Creepy Castle, you would have been trained to use magic properly. As you failed, you cannot use *any* magic ever again. Do you understand me?"

"Never?" A strange feeling of emptiness curled inside me – the same hollow thud I get sometimes when I wake up after dreaming about Mum and Dad. For a moment, everything always seems perfect; then I open my eyes and I remember I'm an orphan and Mum and Dad are never coming back. "No spells at all?" I asked, swallowing hard.

"No spells, no potions, no chants, no charms, no incantations, no hexes," said Aunt Hemlock. "Hold out your wand and shout: *Adieu.*"

"A-dew?" As soon as I said it, the wand leapt out of my hands, wriggled in mid-air, and turned into an enormous brown rat with sharp yellow teeth and a long pink tail.

"Eek," it squeaked as it scurried through the fence, towards the cold grey house next door.

"So you really *were* a rat," I whispered. "I always thought you might be." But the wand was gone.

As I turned back, picking the last jagged splinter out of my finger, the hollow feeling inside me grew deeper. I've never actually got a spell right in my whole life ... so it wasn't *magic* exactly that I'd miss (nor my grumpy old wand). But there was a feeling I got every time I waved my wand or muttered a chant. A little fizz of excitement. A tiny tingle of hope that the magic might just go right. I don't suppose I'll ever feel that tingle again.

"You will be a boring, non-magic Person from now on," said Aunt Hemlock firmly. "It really shouldn't be too difficult; it's not as if you were ever any use in the Magic Realm."

"Useless as a leaky cauldron!" grinned Wane, laughing so hard he flashed like a set of Christmas lights (the Sellwell Department Store Catalogue pages 198–204).

They were right of course. But my heart was pounding – a magical life, living in Aunt Hemlock's cave, is all I had ever known.

"Stand back and leave the magic to me," said Aunt Hemlock as her wand spat sparks. "These silly Persons wished for a child… Well, they should be careful what they wish for."

POOF!

Suddenly Aunt Hemlock was wearing a purple suit.

"There! Now I look like a smart busyness Person," she grinned. "All I need is a handybag… Ah, Wane."

"No, mistress, not me!" He ducked behind a flowerpot, but it was too late.

Pow!

Aunt Hemlock grabbed him by the tail, turned him into a lizard-skin handbag and hung him over her shoulder. "It's only for a little while."

"Ha!" I grinned, but then she spun around and pointed her wand at me.

Ping!

"Dingley daises!" I gasped. "I look like … like Gretel." I was now wearing a brown dress and an apron.

"Exactly! From the fairy tale," beamed Aunt Hemlock. "That is how Person children should look." She must have read me the story of Hansel and Gretel a thousand times when I was little.

"That poor, sweet old hag," tutted Aunt Hemlock. "Roasted in her own oven by those greedy children." She grabbed my shoulder and pushed me towards the cottage. "Never let these Persons know you are a witch — not unless you want to be roasted too," she grinned.

She stretched her long green fingernail and rang the doorbell. "Let the fun and games begin…"

Chapter Six

A light flicked on in a window of the cottage.

"Coming!" called a sleepy voice inside.

"Smile!" hissed Aunt Hemlock, poking me in the ribs.

I nearly toppled over in surprise. Aunt Hemlock had never asked me to look cheerful before — she usually tells me off when I look happy.

"Persons like it when you smile," she

explained. Unfortunately, her twisted sneer didn't look very friendly...

"Can I help you?" A jolly-looking man, as tall as a baby giant, stood in the doorway blinking. "Yikes!" He took one look at Aunt Hemlock and jumped backwards, nearly bumping his bald head and tripping over his enormous feet, which were stuffed inside a pair of very small, fluffy pink slippers.

"Ladies' So-Soft Cosy Toes – candyfloss colour!" I gasped.

"What?" Aunt Hemlock scowled at me.

"They – er – belong to my wife," blushed the man.

"I couldn't find mine anywhere." He looked down at his feet and smiled. "I think I like these better anyway … mine are ever so boring and brown."

"They're brilliant!" I smiled too (and not because Aunt Hemlock had told me to). I knew at once that I liked this funny Person with no hair on his head. I liked the way his shoulders shook as he laughed at himself (Aunt Hemlock only ever laughed at other people).

"Mr Able?" Aunt Hemlock was grinning like a Halloween pumpkin. "I am from FAKE."

"Fake?" Mr Able looked confused.

"*I told you Persons were stupid*," whispered Aunt Hemlock from behind her hand. "We are a charity," she said, talking slowly so that Mr Able could understand. "F-A-K-E. It stands for Fostering and Adopting Kids

Easily. You and your wife did want to foster a child, didn't you?"

"Well … er, yes." Mr Able scratched his head. "But we only phoned the council yesterday. We haven't even had a meeting yet. They said it would take months to put everything in place." He turned and smiled kindly at me. "Although, we would be delighted if things moved quicker than that."

"Well they *have* moved quicker," said Aunt Hemlock, shuffling her papers. "Much quicker. You said you'd be happy to take even the most hopeless case." Aunt Hemlock pointed at me. "Well, they don't come any more hopeless than this."

"I'm sure that's not true," said Mr Able, frowning.

"Hmm, you'll find out soon enough," sighed Aunt Hemlock. "Her name is Belladon—"

"Bella – just Bella." I stepped forward. If I was going to start a new life I might as well start it with a name I liked. "I'm Bella Broomstick," I grinned.

"Pleased to meet you, Bella."

Mr Able held out his hand. I wasn't sure why, so I just smiled even harder than before. "Pleased to meet you too."

"Broomstick is an unusual-sounding name," he said.

"Not where I come from," I answered, thinking how much worse it could have been.

Surnames at the Toadstool Spell Group

(of course!)

Addertongue	Frogfeet	Newtbreath
Batburn	Lizardlegs	Pustule-Pimpleton
Cauldronhead	McEggsmell	Vonvomit

Aunt Hemlock dropped her pile of papers into Mr Able's outstretched hand. "You'll find these all in order," she said. "Now, if you'll excuse me, I must fly…"

"But … hold on a moment." Poor Mr Able stared down at the papers. Beads of sweat appeared on his bald brow. "This all seems most unusual. I mean, you turning up in the middle of the night and everything… I … I'll call my wife." He stepped back into the house and hollered up the stairs. "Rose! There's a lady here says she's from something or other FAKE. She's got a little nipper for us—"

ZAP! The minute he turned his back Aunt Hemlock froze him like a statue. She clicked her fingers and leapt on to her hovering broomstick. She was already in her old witchy clothes again and Wane was no longer a handbag.

"That was horrible," he choked, coughing up a coin.

"Stop moaning," said Aunt Hemlock, "or I'll leave you here in the Person World too."

"No!" Wane clung to the broomstick. "Anything but that..."

"Here! Look after this." Aunt Hemlock thrust the tiny glass jar into my hand and muttered an incantation:

Take this jar which holds the hopes
Of these silly Person dopes.
Safe and sound the moth must stay,
Or its power will fade away.

"It's so *sparkly*!" I said, holding the jar up in the light from the porch. I had never seen such pretty magic before – most of Aunt Hemlock's potions are gloopy and gassy like bubbling mud. But the moth's wings glistened with the dreams it had carried out of Honeysuckle Cottage.

"Careful!" snapped Aunt Hemlock. "When I trapped the moth, I tricked these fools into thinking they wanted a hopeless child like you. But, if the jar breaks, the spell will be broken..."

"You mean, if the hope moth escapes, these Persons won't want to look after me any more?" I asked.

"Precisely! You'd be no more welcome here than you are in the Magic Realm," laughed Aunt Hemlock.

Wane giggled.

"And remember, Persons don't do magic – so there'll be none of your hopeless hocus-pocus either," snarled Aunt Hemlock. "If any Persons in this village find out you are a witch, they'll throw you into a dungeon. Then they'll start poking their wartless noses through the Curtain of Invisibility."

"Yes, Aunt." I thought of the angry man in the big grey house, shouting about the police. Perhaps I'd be better off without any more magic after all. It had only ever caused me trouble. I took a step towards the warm orange lights of Honeysuckle Cottage.

"I think I'm going to like it here," I said.

"Ha! I wouldn't get your hopes up," cackled Aunt Hemlock, shooting into the sky. "You were a hopeless witch, and you'll be a hopeless Person too…"

PING!

With that she was gone. Not even a "goodbye".

Before I could blink, Mr Able leapt back to life. "So sorry. Strangest feeling," he said, wriggling his neck. "Like I fell asleep on my feet…" He turned and hollered up the stairs. "Rose, are you coming down?"

My legs were shaking like a bowl of newt-eye trifle. This was it — the start of my brand-new life.

I found a pencil! Look, no more spolodges.

Chapter Seven

I stood on the doormat as Mrs Able came bustling down the stairs. She was as round and rosy as an apple.

"What did you pinch my slippers for, you daft noodle," she said, swapping with her husband so that she had her own fluffy pink ones back.

I quickly scanned the sky, checking that Aunt Hemlock really was gone. Thank goodness nobody seemed to have noticed her flying away on her broomstick. I slipped the little shining jar safely into my frilly apron pocket, crossing my fingers and wishing with all my heart that the magic power of the hope moth would be enough to let me stay here.

"It's all a bit peculiar." Mr Able was bobbing around like a boiled egg in a pan of water as he tried to explain about the strange lady from FAKE.

"That's as may be, but don't leave the poor mite standing on the doorstep," said Mrs Able, tutting at her husband. "Come on in, pet, before you grow roots out there." She stepped forward and gathered me up in a strawberry-scented hug. I didn't know anyone could smell so good – no rotten eggs, no garlic, no cheesy feet or swamp mud.

"It's Bella, is it?" said Mrs Able, whisking me through to a soft pink room that she said was called the "lounge".

"Yes, Mrs Able." I was so overcome, I bobbed down on one knee, holding the frilly hem of my Gretel dress as if I was meeting a queen.

"That's quite enough of that!" said Mrs Able.

"Sorry!" I was worried that I'd made her cross. But, when I looked up, I saw she was smiling harder than ever.

"Call me Rose," she said. "Or Rosie … or whatever you like. Just not Mrs Able. It makes me feel as if I am in the queue at the doctor's."

"Eew!" I shuddered at the thought of the old witch doctor back in the Magic Realm with his cave full of crocodile teeth and pickled eyes in jars. "May I call you Aunty Rose?" I asked.

"Of course!" Mrs Able's apple cheeks

YUK!

flushed pink. "Although, I am not your real aunt," she said quickly. "It is important you understand that."

"Oh, yes!" I nodded hard. I already had a real aunt and I didn't want any more of those.

"I'd better be Uncle Martin, then," said Mr Able, holding up his left hand. "High five?"

"Er…" Yet again, I had no idea what I was meant to do. Persons are stranger than I thought. "High five!" I waved at him and wiggled my fingers in the air.

"Righty-ho!" Uncle Martin laughed and wiggled his fingers back. "Welcome to the family, Bella. We've waited a long time to meet someone as special as you."

"Oh, I'm not special," I said. "I couldn't even get into Creepy Castle School. Just ask Nightshade Newtbreath..." I trailed off, remembering I wasn't supposed to tell them anything about coming from the Magic Realm.

"Well, I don't know who this Newty Nightbreath is," said Aunty Rose, laying her hand gently on my shoulder, "but you're very special to *us*. We couldn't have children of our own, you see ... so we're bound to spoil you rotten."

"Rotten?" My heart sank. I should have known there would be rot and mould if Aunt Hemlock was involved. Though I couldn't see any. The room was spotlessly clean –

especially the big shiny screen in the corner.

"Do you like a bit of telly?" asked Uncle Martin.

"Er, yes please ... but only a small portion," I said quickly. I hoped *telly* didn't taste like Aunt Hemlock's maggot-mush stew. Uncle Martin and Aunty Rose exchanged a glance and I knew at once that I'd got it wrong.

"Pickled porcupines, I've said something silly, haven't I?" I blushed. "Telly ... *Telly*-vision, of course." They were talking about the big black screen. I had seen pictures of them in the Sellwell catalogue (pages 242–259), but I had no idea what they were for.

"Nonsense." Aunty Rose took my arm. "It's no wonder you're thinking about food. You must be starving. Why don't I run you a nice hot bath while Uncle Martin makes you some breakfast?"

"Good idea. I'm starving too," said Uncle

Martin, stretching sleepily. "Though I don't know why. It's still only half past five in the morning."

I glanced out the window. A pale summer dawn was creeping over the garden.

"It is strange you were brought to us in the middle of the night," said Aunty Rose as she led me up the stairs. "I'll give the council a ring when their offices open."

I wondered if the council was like the coven of witches who meet every full moon to decide on new punishments. A terrible thought struck me. "Will the council be able to send me away?"

"Don't you worry about a thing," said Uncle Martin. "The lady from FAKE said it would all work like magic!"

"Yes, like *magic*," I agreed, curling my hands around the hope-moth jar in my apron pocket. I realized Aunt Hemlock would hex the council too. But, suddenly, I didn't care what sort of cunning spells she had cast across the Person World – just so long as I got to stay.

Aunty Rose led me to a pretty little room with blue-and-white tiles and pictures of dolphins on the walls. She began to run clear, clean water into a sparkling white bath. Steam rose up and clouded the window.

"Hot water!" I gasped. I was only ever allowed a proper bath (rather than a squelch in the swamp) once a year – in the freezing sheep trough at Halloween.

"And a real toilet!" I dashed forward and peered inside the deep bowl. "What happens if I pull this?" I tugged at the little silver handle on the side. "Jiggling jellyfish!" I cried as a whooshing whirlpool swirled underneath me.

"Goodness!" laughed Aunty Rose. She was

looking at me very strangely. "How about some bubbles? Then I'll leave you to it."

Five minutes later, I was soaking in a warm, bubbly peach-smelling bath. "Who says Persons can't do magic," I grinned, sinking down so that only my nose was poking out above the foam. "Aunt Hemlock could learn a thing or two."

Chapter Eight

I lay in the bubbly bath so long, my skin turned as wrinkly as a toad's kneecaps. "Don't you dare laugh!" I said, poking my soggy finger at the steamed-up mirror above the sink.

The mirror said nothing.

"Of course!" I smiled, drying myself on a snowy-white towel. "You can't talk, can you? You're just an ordinary mirror. Not a magic one at all."

I wiped the glass and peered at my reflection. For the first time ever, I was pleased I didn't have any hairy green warts on my nose. Uncle Martin and Aunty Rose didn't have any either.

"If only I didn't have to wear these silly clothes. They're definitely not right for the Person World," I sighed, climbing back into the Gretel costume. I slipped my hand inside the apron pocket, checking the tiny hope-moth jar was still safe.

Then I flushed the toilet again (twice), just for fun!

Aunt Hemlock's spell must have been a pretty powerful one. By the time I came downstairs, Aunty Rose had phoned the council. They sounded surprised but confirmed that all the paperwork to foster Miss B. Broomstick (me!) had been filed. Everything was in order. As long as the hope-moth stayed safely inside its jar, I would be able to stay here for ever. I did a dance of joy and my frilly apron flew up in the air.

"I think we'd better get you some new clothes," laughed Aunty Rose, as if she had understood my deepest wish. "You can't wear that funny thing all the time." She looked me up and down. "How about a little shopping trip?"

"Shopping?" A thousand fireworks exploded in my tummy. "Like the Sellwell Department Store Catalogue?"

"Catalogue?" smiled Aunty Rose. "We can do even better than that!"

"Breakfast first," ordered Uncle Martin, popping his head around the kitchen door. "Is there anything you don't like to eat, Bella?"

"Well … I'm not too fond of frogspawn porridge," I said, shyly.

"Frogspawn?" Uncle Martin and Aunty Rose threw back their heads and laughed. "You are funny," they said.

Uncle Martin made boiled eggs – not rotten ones like Aunt Hemlock cooks, and we didn't have to eat the shells either.

Aunt Hemlock's breakfast (yuk!)

Uncle Martin's breakfast (YUMMY!)

"Ready?" said Aunty Rose when I had eaten every yummy crumb. She grabbed her handy bag (as Aunt Hemlock would call it). "We need to go into town. That's where the fancy shops are."

"Jumping jawbones!" I was so excited, my feet barely touched the ground as we stepped out of the front door.

"I'll stay here," said Uncle Martin. "I want to build a new nesting box for my birds."

Aunty Rose raised her eyebrows. "He's bird-barmy!" she whispered. "Spends every minute cooing and clucking around the garden, as if he had feathers himself."

I smiled and turned to wave goodbye, when I heard a noise like a screaming banshee coming down the road.

"Sounds like a police siren," said Aunty Rose.

"They're heading next door to Hawk Hall

again." Uncle Martin pointed to the huge grey house I had seen last night. There was a screech of wheels and a flash of blue light as a bright white vehicle skidded to a stop outside the tall iron gates.

"A car!" I whispered to myself. "So they really are real. Look!" I cried as a tiny,

terrified kitten darted around the side of
the big grey house and scurried away.

"Poor little thing. It'll be in trouble if Mr
Seymour sees it." Aunty Rose pointed to a
sign hanging on the spiky railings:

HAWK HALL
PRIVATE PROPERTY
KEEP OUT!

"Mr Seymour does not like trespassers …
not even cats," she said as the gates swung
open and the police car drove through.

"Surely the poor little kitten isn't doing
any harm?" I said.

"No." Uncle Martin shook his head. "Mr
Seymour claims he saw something flying

over the village..."

"Last night?" I asked. My heart pounded as I remembered how the man had shouted at us when we flew over on Aunt Hemlock's broomstick.

"Apparently he called the police right away but they said he'd have to wait until morning," explained Uncle Martin.

"Mr Seymour is forever calling them about something," said Aunty Rose. "He thought he saw an alien spaceship last week. And what was it before that?"

"A flying carpet," chuckled Uncle Martin.

I held my breath as two Police Persons stepped out of the car. Were they looking for me? Did they already know I was a witch?

But they turned towards us with a friendly wave. I was relieved to see they had two eyes each and were only half the size of the giant Cyclops Cops back in the Magic Realm.

"What exactly did Mr Seymour say he saw in the sky?" I asked, my tummy churning like a bubbling cauldron. The Police Persons might look friendly but they still had metal handcuffs on their belts.

"Have a guess," smiled Uncle Martin. "You'll never believe it."

"Er... Maybe a witch?" I squeaked. "On a broomstick?"

"Well I never!" nodded Uncle Martin. "Spot on!"

"You're a smart one!" said Aunty Rose.

And they both stared at me in surprise, yet again.

Chapter Nine

We left Merrymeet village and drove to town ... on a bus! The journey took ages but I didn't mind. There were so many new Persons to look at, and not one of them had a wobbly green wart. (I tried not to stare at them *too* much.)

We wound along the country roads, past a big white windmill on a hill. I was so busy looking at all the different Persons, I almost didn't notice that we had arrived in town.

"This is us," said Aunty Rose, stepping off the bus. "Stay close — I don't want you getting lost!"

I had never been anywhere so crowded in all my life. There were hundreds of Persons hurrying along the street. I felt I might be lifted up and carried away like a stick in a stream.

The tall buildings were big and black and as shiny as beetle wings. Then we turned the corner and I stopped as still as if I'd been frozen by a spell.

Ahead of us was a big silver building, seven stories high with shining windows on every floor.

"SELLWELL DEPARTMENT STORE!" I gulped, reading the giant letters above the door. "It's not just a catalogue ... it's a real shop."

"Of course," grinned Aunty Rose. "Shall we go in?"

As we walked up to the big glass doors, they opened all by themselves, as if someone had waved a magic wand. "How did that happen?" I asked. But, before Aunty Rose could answer, I grabbed her hand again. "Look!" I pointed to a big display in the window.

And there … right in the middle … was the fabulous, feathery flamingo pen.

"That's my very favourite thing in the whole Sellwell catalogue," I grinned. I couldn't believe I was seeing it in real life!

"It is lovely," laughed Aunty Rose, leading me into the shop.

She had to keep pulling me along as I stopped to stare at all the wonderful treasures on display.

"There's the escalator," said Aunty Rose and we stepped on to a flight of moving steps. "We need the fourth floor."

"Wondrous Wizards!" Without even moving our feet, we were carried up to the children's clothes department. If we had been in the Magic Realm, I would have thought someone had put an enchantment on the stairs.

"You are going to need some everyday things," said Aunty Rose. "And some underwear and pyjamas too."

I couldn't believe all the brightly coloured clothes. Everybody in the Magic Realm always wore black and grey. And there were no cloaks or pointy hats here either.

In the end, I think I must have tried on just about everything in the shop, but this is what we chose:

My favourite was the pyjamas. "Can I wear them home?" I asked.

"Not in the street," smiled Aunty Rose. I was never going to understand all the rules of the Person World!

I put on shorts and a blue T-shirt instead. "Crazy crocodiles!" I said, jumping up and down in my new shoes. "These are the comfiest things I have ever worn."

Old clothes

New clothes

Proper Person clothes at last!

"Good," said Aunty Rose. "And what about this?" She pointed to my Gretel dress with the frilly apron which was in a tangled heap on the changing room floor.

"Hmm," I wrinkled my nose.

"We could save it for dressing up?" smiled Aunty Rose. "Or give it to the jumble…"

"What's the jumble?" I asked. It sounded like the terrible mixed-up monster who lives in the bottom of Aunt Hemlock's well…

"A jumble sale. Fancy not knowing what

Jumble Monster!

that is!" Aunty Rose looked at me strangely. "What a funny old life you must have lived," she said. "It's almost like you're from another planet." Then she blushed. "I'm sorry, pet. I don't mean to pry. I am sure you'll tell me more about it when you're ready. A jumble sale is somewhere you sell things you don't want any more. There's a sale in the village today, in aid of the Merrymeet children's playground."

"Brilliant." If someone else liked the Gretel dress, they were welcome to it. "I never want to see it again," I said, digging my hands deep into the pockets of my new shorts. At last, I was beginning to look like all the other Persons I had seen.

"I'll go and pay and meet you in the cafe," smiled Aunty Rose. "There's just one more thing I need to do."

I stuffed the old Gretel dress into a bag

and hurried to the cafe.

When Aunty Rose arrived, as well as the shopping bags of clothes, she was carrying a tiny pink paper bag and was smiling from ear to ear. "Now," she said, "how about an ice cream before we head home?"

"Laughing ladybirds!" I grinned, licking ice cream off my spoon. If only Nightshade Newtbreath could see me now. Here I was sitting in the cafe at the Sellwell Department Store, wearing cool summer clothes and eating food so delicious it made my tongue tingle. Life in the Person World couldn't be more perfect!

Magic!

My drawings are about to get SO much better – you'll never guess why!

Chapter Ten

The bus stopped when we passed the old white windmill on the way home. A mother with a baby climbed on board and two girls followed her. The youngest was only tiny – but the older one looked about the same age as me.

She smiled at me as she walked past, holding her little sister by the hand. She had honey-coloured hair in a ponytail and freckles on her nose (not a single hairy wart or green tooth, of course).

The whole family wore clothes with pretty patterns on them, stripes and stars and flowers all mixed up together. Their outfits were nothing like my new clothes or any of the other things I had seen in the Sellwell Department Store. Some of the colours were a little faded and there were patches stitched on here and there, but they all looked so cheerful it made me grin. The baby was dressed like a bumblebee and I could hear bells tinkling on the bottom of the older girl's skirt.

"Come on!" she said, swinging her little sister on to the back seat. They all clapped their hands and sang a song about "The Wheels on the Bus".

I wished I was brave enough to join in — the two sisters were laughing so much. I thought how much fun it would be to make a friend now I was living in the Person

World. The smiling older girl looked a LOT nicer than Nightshade Newtbreath!

The singing stopped when we got near Merrymeet village. The girl pressed her face against the window as if she was looking for something she had lost.

I wished I could ask her what was wrong but, all of a sudden, I saw the white chimney of Honeysuckle Cottage and the tall spiked fence of Hawk Hall.

Aunty Rose rang a bell. "Time to get off the bus," she said. "We're home."

I ran straight upstairs to my very own pretty pink bedroom with roses on the wallpaper. Aunty Rose said it used to be the spare room, but it could be mine from now on.

I unpacked all my new clothes and put them in the chest of drawers. I was just hanging up my dressing gown when Aunty Rose popped her head round the door.

"Leaping lizards!" I nearly jumped out of my skin. For a minute I thought she might be a Police Person coming to arrest me after all.

"Sorry to startle you," she smiled, holding out the tiny paper bag she had got in the Sellwell Department Store. "But I just wanted to give you one more thing."

"For me?" I stared at the little bag. It was far too small for another jumper or a pair of shoes, and I had enough knickers and socks for every day of the week.

"Go on," said Aunty Rose. "Aren't you going to open it?"

"Can I?" I took the bag and peeped inside. "It's…" Suddenly I couldn't speak. My throat was too tight. My fingers were shaking like a dragonfly's wings.

"Oh, pet. Did I do something wrong?" Aunty Rose wrapped her arm around me. "It's just a little treat from me and Uncle Martin … to say welcome to our home."

"But … it's the flamingo pen." I held it up. It was fluffy and feathery and pink and perfect. "Thank you! It's the most wonderful gift I could ever wish for!"

"It's only a little pen," smiled Aunty Rose. I stroked the fluffy feathers against my cheek. "It's the nicest thing anyone has ever done for me!"

"You poor lamb." Aunty Rose made a big wet gulping sound like a foot stuck in mud. She turned away quickly but I saw she had tears in her eyes.

"You should go down and show Uncle Martin the pen," she sniffed, pointing towards the garden. "I know he'd love to see it."

"All right," I agreed, wondering how I had upset her so much. But she wiped her eyes and smiled as broadly as ever.

"He's out there seeing to his birds, as usual," she laughed. "Not that there'll be anything as exotic as a flamingo in our garden, of course."

"I better show him this one then," I said, waving the pen in the air as I dashed down the stairs.

"I'll pop down to the village," Aunty Rose

called after me. "The jumble sale will be open now. There's just time to drop off that old dress of yours, if you are sure you don't want it."

"Positive," I shouted over my shoulder. I never wanted to see that silly, frilly Gretel dress ever again.

Chapter Eleven

Uncle Martin was standing beside the bird table at the bottom of the garden. "Shoo!" he cried, waving his arms as I ran towards him. For a moment I thought he was talking to me. Then I spotted the same fluffy grey kitten I had seen running away from the Police Persons this morning.

The naughty creature leapt towards the bird table and clung on by one paw. A flock of sparrows shot into the sky tweeting in terror.

"Stop that!" cried Uncle Martin.

"You cheeky little rascal!" I hissed under my breath in Cat Chat as the ball of grey fluff jumped to the ground.

"Rascal! I like that name," he purred, puffing himself up to twice his fluffy size. "I think it suits me!"

"Well then, Rascal, just you leave those birds alone," I said, crouching down so that only the kitten could hear me. I knew enough about the Person World to know that it wasn't normal to hiss and purr as if you are having a proper conversation with a cat.

"Shoo!" Uncle Martin charged towards the kitten flapping an empty packet of sunflower seeds. Rascal shot away through the shiny black railings of Hawk Hall.

"No! Don't send him that way," I cried, thinking of mean Mr Seymour. I ran to the fence and peered through. It was too late. The kitten had vanished.

"Don't worry. I expect the mother cat is around here somewhere. He's too young to be out on his own," said Uncle Martin, pouring peanuts into a feeder. "We can't look after every waif and stray. No matter how much we might want to."

"No," I said. But my heart sank. Did he mean me? Was I a waif and stray? Did Uncle

Martin wish that he could shoo me away like the kitten?

I looked up at his gentle, smiling face and couldn't believe that it was true. He had only shooed away the kitten to protect his beloved birds.

"So, what's this magnificent plumage I see?" He pointed to the pink feathers poking out of my hand. I had almost forgotten I was going to show him the pen. "Has a far-flung flamingo found its way to my feeding table?" he grinned. "I'll have to put out prawns as well as peanuts if that's true."

"Ha!" I tried to smile. But I kept thinking how it was all a trick. The Ables wouldn't even have taken me in if not for the spell Aunt Hemlock cast on them.

"Flamingoes love to eat prawns. That's why their feathers turn pink," said Uncle Martin. "I don't know what this lot would make of it, though." He pointed to the flock of sparrows who were back at the bird table, flapping in mid-air as they pecked at a hanging feeder of full of seeds.

The moment I saw their beating wings, I thought of the fluttering hope moth in the jar. "Dizzy demons!" The precious magic creature was still tucked inside my Gretel dress. It was in the frilly apron pocket.

How could I have been so stupid?

Aunty Rose was going to take it to the jumble sale...

Chapter Twelve

"Sorry, Uncle Martin, I – I've got to go!"
I gasped.

Aunt Hemlock had warned me to keep
the moth safe. If the jar was broken, the
magic would be gone and the Ables wouldn't
want me any more.

I dashed back towards the cottage. If only I
could stop Aunty Rose before she left. "Hello?"
I cried. "Aunty Rose? Are you still there?"

"You just missed her," said Uncle Martin,

catching me up. "I saw her set off five minutes ago with a bundle of clothes for the jumble."

"Groaning ghouls!" Why did I tell her I never wanted to see the Gretel dress again? I should have remembered the precious jar was in the apron pocket.

I darted to the hedge and peered along the road but there was no sign of Aunty Rose anywhere.

Uncle Martin looked out of the gate. "Has she taken something of yours by mistake?" he asked.

"Yes!" I wished I could tell him what it was, but I couldn't. If he knew he had been tricked into fostering me, he would call the council and send me away.

"Don't look so worried," he smiled. "We can catch up with Rose in no time. She'll be heading for the jumble sale in the church hall, but she's bound to stop for a gossip at the post office first." He picked up the empty packet of birdseed he had shaken at Rascal. "You go on ahead," he said, pointing down the lane. "Follow the pavement past Hawk Hall and see if you can still see her. If not, wait on the corner for me. I'm just going to fetch my wallet so I can buy some more birdseed while we're in the village."

He bustled back to the cottage as I dashed out of the gate, still holding my flamingo pen. The village lane was completely different from the streets in town. There were no Persons anywhere … and no sign of Aunty Rose either. I hurried along the pavement beside the high railings of Hawk Hall and poked my head around the corner. Nothing! Just two fat ducks on the village pond.

As I waited for Uncle Martin, I peered through the railings into the garden of Hawk

Hall. There wasn't a flower, or even a single blade of grass, anywhere to be seen. In fact, it wasn't really a garden at all.

I paced up and down. What was taking him so long? I still wasn't sure exactly what a jumble sale was, but it didn't sound like a safe place for a delicate moth. If the jar broke, the little creature would fly off, taking its clever magic away for ever. I was just edging a little further around the corner, when I heard a tiny voice cry out in Cat Chat.

"Stop it! Let me go!" It sounded like the fluffy grey kitten … and he was in some sort of trouble.

"Rascal?" I cried, answering in Cat Chat. "Rascal? Where are you?"

"Ouch!" he wailed. "Help me!" His voice was coming from Hawk Hall.

I glanced one last time towards the village. Every moment that passed put the moth in danger but I couldn't just ignore Rascal's cries.

I sped back around the corner and pressed my face against the iron railings. A tall, mean-looking boy, as skinny as a worm, was standing on the driveway and holding Rascal by the scruff of the neck.

Bow tie

"Stop that!" I cried, shouting through the bars. "Put that poor little cat down!"

"Who are you?" The boy marched towards me, swinging the kitten in the air.

Smart suit

"I'm Bella Broomstick. I live next door," I said.

Shiny shoes

"Ah. The new foster brat," the boy wrinkled his pointy nose as if he had

104

a horrid smell underneath it. "Daddy told me all about you. Well, I'm Piers Seymour and my father is the richest man in this village. I don't have to listen to anything you say."

I remembered how happy I had been when the girl with the colourful clothes smiled at me on the bus. But it was obvious not all the children in the Person World were kind. *Bullies are just the same here as in the Magic Realm*, I thought.

Person World bully

Magical Realm bully

NO DIFFERENCE!

"Can't breathe," choked Rascal as Piers squeezed him by the neck.

"Don't worry!" I mewed softly in Cat Chat. "I'll save you, I promise…"

"You're mad." Piers almost dropped the little kitten on his head. "First you try and boss me around. Now you're talking to a cat."

"No I'm not," I said quickly. I should have been more careful. I knew speaking animal languages in the Person World wasn't normal.

"I heard you," Piers laughed. "You were purring at him … it was weird!"

"I was only playing around," I said. "Please. Can't you just let the kitten go?"

"He's trespassing!" Piers waved Rascal wildly in the air and pointed to the PRIVATE PROPERTY notice on the gate. "Nobody trespasses on Seymour land." Rascal wriggled like a fish on a hook.

"He's only a little kitten!" I roared. "Put him down!"

"Make me!" sneered Piers, safe behind his high iron fence.

If only I still had my magic wand, I'd teach this bully a lesson. But the only thing in my hand was the fluffy flamingo pen. "If this was a wand, I'd turn you into a real live worm, Piers Seymour," I muttered under my breath, waving my pen in the air (three times). "That would stop you bullying helpless little creatures once and for all."

Swish! Swish! Swish!

Poof!

There was a loud explosion. I almost fell over backwards as a puff of purple smoke shot out of the end of the biro.

"Galloping Goblins! I didn't expect that to happen," I gasped. My fingers tingled as

I stared at the pen in my hand.

It really *was* a magic wand.

Chapter Thirteen

Rascal dived through the railings and leapt into my arms.

"That was amazing!" he wheezed, still coughing and spluttering from where Piers had squeezed his neck. "You saved me from the bully."

"But ... but..." As the smoke cleared, I stared at the tiny pink worm wiggling across the driveway. "Look what I've done to Piers Seymour!"

There was no mistaking it, the worm *was* Piers — it was still wearing his red bow tie.

"You taught him a lesson, that's for sure!" said Rascal. "How does that thing work?" He stared at the flamingo pen in my shaking fingers.

"It … it's a magic wand," I said slowly, though I still couldn't quite believe it was true. "I waved the pen three times and…"

"Wow!" Rascal's big green eyes grew even wider. "You must be very, very magical," he said.

"Me? I'm not magical at all," I laughed. "I'm hopeless."

But my brain fizzed and a smile spread across my face. I had done proper magic all by myself — and it had worked!

"That's the first time in my whole life I've *ever* got a spell right," I grinned. "If I'd managed that in the Creepy Castle exam,

Dr Rattlebone would have been seriously impressed." Then the truth hit me like a charging bull. This wasn't an exam. My worm wasn't a shoelace. It was a boy.

The smile vanished from my face. "Now what am I going to do? I've just turned Mr Seymour's son into a worm!"

I glanced up and down the road but there was no sign of either Aunty Rose or Uncle Martin. Nor any Police Persons, thank goodness. If any Persons found out I had cast a spell, they'd toss me into prison and throw away the key — for ever. The Ables would never want me back; it wouldn't matter if I managed to save the hope moth or not.

"Don't look so worried," said Rascal, rubbing himself against my ankles. "You were only being kind."

It was true, but I wasn't sure the Ables would see it the same way ... or Piers. The worm wiggled its head angrily from side to side.

"Can't you just wave your wand and change him back again?" asked Rascal.

"I'm not sure," I said. "But I'll have to give it a go!" My only hope was that Piers's worm brain was so tiny, he'd have no idea what was going on. If I could just turn him back into a boy, he might forget any of it had ever happened.

"Here goes," I said, raising the fluffy pink pen. "Become Piers Seymour!" I said firmly, swooshing the pen in a circle three times.

Swish! Swish! Swish!

"Thundering ferrets! That doesn't look right." The tiny worm shot into the air with his little bow tie spinning round. "Sorry, Piers!" I cried as he began to loop the loop.

At that moment, an enormous black crow swooped over the fence from Honeysuckle

Cottage. "Yum! I've never seen a flying worm before," cawed the hungry bird.

"He's going to eat Piers!" I cried, waving my arms wildly at the crow. "Shoo! Go away!"

Rascal dived back through the fence, spitting like a baby leopard. But the crow was almost twice as big as he was. It swooped down, opened his sharp black beak and scooped Piers up in mid-air.

"Stop!" I cried, barking at him in Crow Call (which sounds like a hyena with a bad cough). "You can't eat that. It's not really a worm, it's a boy."

Rascal leapt in the air, trying to grab the crow's feet, but the cunning bird flapped higher. He circled above our heads with Piers hanging from his beak like a wriggly pink tongue.

"Drop that worm now, Mr Crow," I cawed.

Suddenly, Rascal stopped jumping and pricked his ears. "Listen."

Cats have very sharp hearing, but I heard it too. A soft purring growl like a tiger cub getting closer and closer.

I glanced past Honeysuckle Cottage along the winding country road that led towards town. Coming into view, at the top of the hill, was an enormous silver car as shiny as a suit of armour.

"That's Piers's parents," gasped the kitten. "They're coming home."

If I didn't manage to turn Piers back right

now, Mr and Mrs Seymour would arrive just in time to see their son being gobbled up by a hungry crow. "Be a boy again! Be a boy! Be a boy!" I cried, waving the pen.

Nothing happened.

The crow made a horrible slurping sound and Piers disappeared further inside his beak.

Chapter Fourteen

The Seymours' silver car was getting closer as the crow circled with tiny, wiggly Piers half-hanging from his beak.

"Trembling toadstools," I groaned. "For the first time in my life I manage to get a spell right and now I can't undo it!"

Even brave little Rascal was panicking. His hair was standing up on end like a fluffy porcupine. "There must be some way you can turn the spell backwards," he said.

"Backwards? Rascal, you're brilliant!" If three swoops of my wand clockwise had turned Piers into a worm, then three swoops widdershins (which is witchy-speak for the other way) might just turn the spell back round.

The crow took another loud slurp and swallowed Piers right up to his bow tie.

Swish! Swish! Swish! I waved the pen widdershins.

Poof!

There was a puff of pale blue smoke and a scream as Piers Seymour (the full-size boy) fell through the sky. The angry crow didn't have a hope of holding him in his beak now.

"What have you done to my worm!" he cawed furiously.

I ought to have magicked a mattress for Piers to fall on ... or given him wings. Luckily, his jacket caught on one of the high spikes of the fence. He was left dangling in mid-air like a piece of washing pegged to a line.

"Eight, nine, ten." I counted his fingers and breathed a sigh of relief. None of them had been left behind in the spell.

Piers looked confused. "Who are you?" he roared at me as the electric gates opened and his parents' car pulled into the driveway. "What am I doing up here?"

Piers seemed to have forgotten everything. Phew!

"I'm Bella Broomstick," I said, scooping Rascal into my arms. "I'm just checking this cheeky kitten doesn't trespass on your property. You know how naughty cats can be."

"Well, don't just stand there," Piers roared, kicking his shiny shoes against the fence. "Get me down. This is an expensive suit."

His parents leapt out of their car and began running towards us.

"Sorry, I've got to go," I said. Rascal was laughing so hard I almost dropped him. I felt all tingly inside. I had got myself (and Piers) into a horrible muddle, but I had got us out of it again … with *MAGIC!*

I almost wished Aunt Hemlock was here so she could see how well I had done. *Almost*… But not really. If she knew I could do spells she might take me back to the Magic Realm. I wanted to stay in the Person World for ever.

Uncle Martin came dashing down the path from Honeysuckle Cottage, waving his wallet. "Sorry, it took me ages to find this," he called.

In a moment of panic I shoved Rascal under my T-shirt. I didn't want Uncle Martin to see I was cuddling the same naughty kitten he had shooed away from his birds. "Stay there and don't scratch me," I hissed in Cat Chat.

But Uncle Martin wasn't even looking at me. He was staring wide-eyed at the railings of Hawk Hall. "What on earth is Piers doing up there?" he gawped.

"Er … I think a bird might have dropped him," I said, truthfully.

"A bird? You're teasing me," laughed Uncle Martin.

But, before I could say another word, Aunty Rose appeared from the direction of the village. Her hands were empty.

"My Gretel costume?" I cried. "Where is it?"

"Don't worry, it's gone to the jumble," she smiled.

"Gone? And the apron too?"

"I gave the whole thing away, just like you wanted," smiled Aunty Rose. She patted my arm, thinking she was being kind. "Whatever is going on here?" she whispered, as Piers howled like a werewolf and Mr Seymour tugged at his dangling legs.

There was a loud ripping sound as his

trousers split in two.

"Oh dear!" mouthed Aunty Rose. Uncle Martin put his hand to his mouth, but he was far too kind to laugh out loud.

"Don't gawp like a couple of goldfish!" snapped Mr Seymour. "Do something to help."

"Of course…" They dashed towards the railings.

"I … I'm going to my room for a bit, if that's all right?" I turned and sped towards the cottage, still clutching Rascal under my T-shirt. I could feel tears pricking my eyes. I glanced nervously at the clear blue sky, half-expecting Aunt Hemlock to appear and whisk me back to the Magic Realm so I could be a guinea pig in the potions lab after all. Everything had gone wrong. I had made a hopeless mess of being in the Person World already.

RULE ONE:
DON'T USE MAGIC.

RULE TWO:
KEEP THE HOPE MOTH SAFE.

BELLA BROOMSTICK SCORE:
FAIL!

Chapter Fifteen

"Just stay under the duvet and don't go poking about," I said as Rascal hung off the end of my bed and tried to peer underneath it.

I knew I shouldn't have brought him inside without asking. But Uncle Martin didn't even want a kitten in the garden, let alone the house. "No more waifs and strays!" That's what he'd said. Well, he wouldn't have to worry about that for much longer. My Gretel dress was gone. The glass jar was probably broken already and the hope moth would have flown away.

I could hear the Ables murmuring in the kitchen below. As soon as they escaped from the power of Aunt Hemlock's spell, they would realize they had never wanted to foster me at all. Perhaps they were already using their strange telephone-thing to call the council and say there had been some mistake.

Rascal stuck his head in the wastepaper basket. "What's in here?" he asked.

"Nothing!" I sighed. "I thought I told you to stop poking about."

"Do another spell," he said, pouncing on the bed as I sat playing with the feathers on my pink flamingo pen. "Do one on me. But I don't want to be a worm." He arched his back. "Turn me into a lion … or a tiger. It will be a very easy spell as I am so big and fierce already."

"Really?" I smiled. I didn't like to tell him he was no bigger than a guinea pig.

"Listen to me roar!" he growled. It was more like the buzz of a bumble bee. "Go on. Wave your wand."

"No more spells!" I lifted my pillow and slid the pen underneath it. "You saw what happened to Piers."

"It was brilliant," said Rascal.

"He was nearly eaten alive by a killer bird!" I groaned.

"Imagine if the poor old crow had choked on his bow tie," giggled Rascal.

"You shouldn't laugh. We were in serious trouble back there." But I couldn't help smiling. It was impossible to be cross – or sad – for long with Rascal around. I slipped my fingers under the pillow and felt the soft feathers of the flamingo pen.

"No! I mustn't." I folded my arms tightly. "Persons do not use magic. And I don't want to either. Magic only ever causes problems. Now, will you *please* get back under the duvet and stop poking about!"

"Oh!" Rascal's ears drooped and his tail sunk between his legs. That's the thing with Cat Chat – you have to hiss and spit when you're being firm, but it makes you sound super-fierce and angry. I must have sounded far more cross than I meant too.

"Mum's always telling me off for being too curious," he mewed. "That's how I got in trouble in the first place."

"What happened?" I purred gently. "Where's your mum now?"

"I'm not sure," said Rascal, burying his head in his paws. "I climbed into a box, just to see what was in there. Then I fell asleep and somebody carried it off. When I woke up, I was in a pile of boxes for the jumble sale at the village hall."

"Horrid jumble! It causes problems for everyone," I said, stoking his ears and imagining a mean kitten-stealing monster wearing my Gretel dress.

"I wriggled out of the box and dashed straight home," sniffed Rascal. "But Mum had gone. So had my brother and sister. And the family we live with."

"Don't worry. I'm sure we can find them," I said.

"How?" mewed Rascal. "I peeped in the window of the flat where we used to live, but everything had vanished. Even the furniture."

"Who'd want to make their furniture vanish?" I said. Persons really are very peculiar. "And how do they do it if they don't use magic?"

"I don't know," wailed Rascal. "If only I hadn't fallen asleep in that silly box. There wasn't even anything to see, just lots of dusty old books. But it was so dark and cosy."

"How did you end up at Hawk Hall?" I asked.

"I saw the broomstick, flying through the sky, with you and the big witch … and the crazy lizard thing."

"Wane," I laughed.

"I wasn't scared. Not one little bit. I decided to follow it," explained the kitten. "Witches like cats, don't they? I thought the big one with the pointy hat might use her magic to help me."

"Oh dear. Aunt Hemlock never helps anyone," I said, stroking his fluffy head.

"That lizard stuck his tongue out at me," said Rascal.

He looked so sad – ever since he had started to talk about his mum, all the puff and fluff had gone out of him. But what could I do?

"I wish I could help. But I don't even know your real name," I said as he curled up on my lap.

"It's Rascal now," he yawned. "You chose it. I never had a proper name before I met you. Mum just calls me Number Three, because she says I am smaller than my brother and sister... But I'm not!"

"Well, Rascal certainly suits you," I said.

"That's because I'm fearless and not afraid of trouble," yawned the tiny kitten, curling up on my lap. "Since you've given me a name, you'll have to help me. Mum says that's what naming a cat means … it's like a promise to look after me."

"But—"

"You are going to help me find her, aren't you?" he said with a happy little snuffling sound. "I knew you would. Do you think you'll use magic? It'll be awesome if you do."

"No magic! I already told you," I said firmly.

But Rascal closed his eyes and laid his head on my knee. He was just starting to snore when there was a knock on my bedroom door.

"This is it," I whispered. "The Ables have realized they were tricked by magic. Now they've come to tell me to leave."

Chapter Sixteen

"Bella?" Aunty Rose rapped on the door firmly.

"One minute," I scrambled to my feet and slipped sleepy Rascal into my half-open sock drawer. "Stay there and don't move," I warned him. Then I opened my bedroom door to face Aunty Rose.

She was holding out a tall glass of something dark and fizzy. The only bubbly black liquid I know is swamp gas, which goes into most of Aunt Hemlock's favourite potions. Surely Aunty Rose wouldn't make me drink anything like that…

"I brought you a glass of cola," she smiled. Cola? Well, that didn't sound too bad…

"And some crisps," she said, handing me a little snack on a plate. "Don't get any crumbs on the bed … and we're going to have to start eating a bit more healthily tomorrow."

"Tomorrow?" I gasped. So they weren't

sending me away? At least not yet. Aunty Rose was still being so kind, bringing me treats. Perhaps there was a chance the jar hadn't broken … the moth was still safe. "Thank you." I sniffed the bubbling black liquid and took a tiny sip. "Fuzzy Fungus!" The *fizz* went right up my nose but it was delicious – like shooting stars and sugar. "Yum!" I took a giant gulp.

"Careful!" Aunty Rose patted me on the back. When I finally finished spluttering, I cleared my throat.

"What would somebody do if they sent something to the jumble by mistake?" I asked.

"This is about that costume of yours, isn't it?" said Aunty Rose, sitting down on the bed beside me.

"Yes," I mumbled. I couldn't bear to make her feel bad for giving the Gretel dress away.

I was the one who had told her to get rid of it in the first place. She wasn't to know I'd left a jar of powerful magic inside the apron pocket.

"There's a good chance it might not have been sold," said Aunty Rose. "Uncle Martin can take you down to the village right now, if you like. He still wants to buy birdseed. But you better be quick." She glanced at her watch. "The jumble sale closes in fifteen minutes."

The jumble sale smelt like Aunt Hemlock's socks. But it was really fun and colourful too. There were piles of clothes and tables of teapots, cups and plates, a barrel of toys and a basket of wellington boots in every shade of the rainbow (though none of them seemed to be a matching pair). Nothing was shiny and crisp and new (like the things in the Sellwell Department Store), but everything seemed as if it had once been loved. Jars of buttons and bottles of beads shimmered like treasure and there were weird things too — a wastepaper basket shaped like an elephant's foot (Aunt Hemlock would have snapped that up) and a giant purple teddy bear as tall as Uncle Martin.

There was a table of tea and coffee, cakes and biscuits and bright-orange squash as well. Aunty Rose had given me a shiny fifty pence which I would have loved to spend on a giant slice of sponge cake stuffed with strawberries and cream, but I had to save the money to buy my Gretel costume back.

"Excuse me," I said, peering over a mountain of winter hats and woolly scarves.

"Hello, dearie," said the old woman running the clothes stall. She was tiny and wrinkly as if she might have tumbled out of a bag of jumble along with the clothes. Her kind brown eyes were as big and round as buttons. "What can I do for you?"

"Well—"

"How about a winter scarf?" She pulled a bright red one from the very bottom of the pile so that all the others tumbled to the floor in an avalanche of wool and bobbles. "It's summer now, but you'll be glad of something cosy come Christmas time."

"No thanks," I said, scrabbling on the floor and piling mittens and gloves back on to the table. "I'm looking for a special outfit. Like a costume."

"Ah!" She began to flick through a rail of clothes. "Cinderella, Belle, Minnie Mouse, Mickey Mouse, a dalmatian, Shrek?"

"No, it's—"

"Father Christmas, Elsa, Superman,

Spiderman – no idea what this one is supposed to be – a witch, a wizard, Alice in Wonderland or—"

"Sorry!" I stood on tiptoes and shouted as loudly as I could. "It's a special costume I'm looking for, you see. Like Gretel from the fairy tale ... brown with a frilly apron on the top."

"Well blow me down!" she grinned toothlessly. "Rose Able came in earlier and donated one just like that."

"That's it!" I cried, holding out my fifty pence. "Please can I buy it back?"

"Sorry!" Her face crumpled like a paper bag. "You just missed it."

"Missed it?" The coin almost slipped from my fingers. "You mean it's been sold."

"That's jumble for you," she sighed. "Hundreds of things that nobody wants and one thing they're all after. Had the same trouble with a clock shaped like a fried egg last year. Mrs Brimblecombe from the post office got quite nasty—"

"The costume," I said, darting round the side of the table so I could see her properly. "Please, it's really important. I don't suppose you noticed, but did it have anything in the pocket?"

"The pocket?"

"Yes."

"The apron pocket?"

"Yes." I felt a surge of hope. Maybe she had seen the jar and kept it safe.

"Sorry, couldn't say."

"Oh!" I sighed.

"I wish I could help but I only had the dress a few minutes, dearie," she explained. "Rose Able had only just dropped it off when the little girl came up. Desperate to have it she was."

"Little girl?" I asked.

"Young Gretel. Her mum used to run the secondhand bookshop," the old lady smiled. "Gretel's her real name — just like in the story. Perhaps that's why she wanted the costume so much."

"I suppose that makes sense," I nodded.

"Don't tell anyone but I let her have it for free," whispered the old lady, leaning forward and taking my hand. "Seemed the least I could do after all the trouble that poor family have had. Mr Seymour throwing them out of their home like that..."

"Mr Seymour?" I asked. "What did he do?"

"He owns the building the family were renting," the old lady explained. "But he closed the bookshop down and threw them out of the flat with just one day's notice. He's going to turn the whole place into fancy

offices for his concrete-making company,
'Seymour Cement'. Now we don't have our
lovely old bookshop any more."

"That's terrible," I said. The more I heard
about the Seymours the more they reminded
me of Aunt Hemlock and her horrid tricks.
I wouldn't be surprised if they grew big
green warts on the end of their noses.

"And little Gretel and her family have

had to leave Merrymeet for good," sighed
the old lady.

"You mean they don't even live in the

village any more?" I asked. My last chance of finding the costume and saving the hope moth was gone.

"They only popped back this morning because they were looking for a lost kitten," the old lady said.

"A kitten?" My heart was racing again.

"They dropped off some books and things," said the old lady. "They think the little grey kitten might have crawled into—"

"Into the box," I cried, flinging my arms around her neck. These were Rascal's owners for sure. "Please. You have to tell me where they've gone."

"That's easy. They've taken shelter in the Old Windmill. Dreadful, draughty place. Can't miss it," she said. "Five miles out of the village on top of the hill."

"I've seen it!" I said. "On the road to town."

"That's the one," smiled the old lady. "Run quick and you might even catch the last bus!"

Chapter Seventeen

"Why can't we go to the windmill right now?" asked Rascal, scratching his claws on the end of my bed. "You could save your magic butterfly and I could see my mum."

"It's a moth," I sighed. "And it's Saturday night, which means there aren't any buses until Monday morning. I missed the last one by a weasel's whisker."

I paced up and down the room. I wished I could help Rascal and I couldn't bear the thought of waiting the whole weekend before I could try and rescue the hope moth.

The lady at the jumble sale said Gretel was only four years old (and very lively). She'd be sure to break the jar or lose it somewhere by Monday.

"If only I could ask the Ables to help," I said, peering out of the window as the last of the day's sun began to fade. "But then I'd have to explain how I brought you into the house without asking." Rascal curled himself around my ankles. "Then they'd get cross and throw us both out."

"But you are a witch," purred Rascal. "Couldn't we just fly to the windmill by broomstick?"

"No!" I said. "No more magic! Anyway, Aunty Rose probably doesn't even have a broomstick." The nearest thing I'd seen was a vacuum cleaner.

"She does," said Rascal. "It's next to the mop in the back of the cupboard beside the stove."

"You've been poking about downstairs!" I cried. "What if you'd been caught? I told you to stay hidden."

"Sorry." Rascal looked up at me with his big green eyes. "I just don't want Mum to worry where I've gone. I never even got to say goodbye to her."

"All right, all right!" I said as he rubbed his head underneath my chin and mewed pitifully. "Anything to get you back home before you cause any real trouble. How long was the broom handle? Do you think we'll both fit?"

Aunty Rose and Uncle Martin had tucked me up in bed hours ago. The cottage was quiet and the garden was dark as Rascal and I slipped out on to the lawn.

"Ready?" I whispered, laying Aunty

Rose's jolly red sweeping brush down on the grass. "Keep out of the way and don't ask any questions."

"Why would I ask questions?" asked Rascal.

"That *is* a question!" I giggled. "Just stand behind me and don't move until I say so. Getting a broomstick to fly is a very tricky spell."

This wasn't true actually. Most witches do it about ten times a day, but I'd never been able to make it happen. Not once!

Things would be different now, I told myself, taking the magical feathery pen from behind my ear. My wand wasn't a grumpy old rat any more – it was a beautiful pink flamingo. "If I can turn Piers Seymour into a wiggly worm and back again, I can make a broomstick fly."

"How fast will we go?" asked Rascal. "Will we be able to touch the moon?"

"Shh!" I held my flamingo wand above the broomstick and muttered the words I had heard other witches say a thousand times:

Sweep like wings into the sky,
Brush the clouds and fly, fly, fl—

Poof!

There was a puff of pink smoke and I shot backwards on to the lawn. Rascal, who was standing right behind me, tumbled too. We rolled across the grass in a tangle of arms, legs and a fluffy tail. "Ouch!" I cried as his claw went up my nose (though I'm sure he didn't mean to scratch me).

"Did it work?" said Rascal, staggering to his feet. "Are we going to fly now?"

I stared at the broomstick lying flat on the grass. "I'm sorry," I groaned. I knew how much Rascal wanted to see his mum. "We're not going anywhere." I was still as hopeless at magic as ever.

"Oh! Have you seen your fluffy wand-thingy?" asked Rascal.

"No," I scrabbled around on the dark grass trying to find the pen. "I must have dropped it somewhere..."

"No. I mean, have you *seen* it? Behind you!" said Rascal. His tail was puffed up to twice its normal size.

Very, *very* slowly, I turned my head. A large pink flamingo – a *real* one – was balancing on one leg, dipping her beak into the bird bath on the edge of the lawn.

"Fluttering feathers! Hello," I gasped, stretching out to stroke the bird's pink plumage. She was beautiful. My broomstick spell might not have worked, but something much more extraordinary had happened instead. "I suppose if my old wooden wand was an angry rat, there is no reason my pen-wand shouldn't be a real flamingo."

"Ark!" squawked the bird.

"Shh!" I put my finger to my lips as a light flickered on in Hawk Hall.

"What's the big birdy-thing saying?" asked Rascal.

"I'm not sure." The bird stretched out her long neck and I stroked the smooth feathers on top of her head. "I don't speak Flamingo." There aren't any beautiful pink birds in the Magic Realm … just crows and owls.

"Ark!" The flamingo flapped her wings.

"I think she wants to fly," I said. But she

bent her knees and tugged at my sleeve with her black-tipped beak. She scooped up Rascal, like a pea on a spoon, and swung him on her back. "She wants us to come with her," I grinned.

"Is she our broomstick?" purred Rascal.

"Yes!" I cried, scrambling on to the flamingo's feathery back as bright lights blazed on all across the concrete gardens of Hawk Hall. "Fly! Fly! Fly!"

Chapter Eighteen

Rascal perched on the flamingo's neck as we flew over the shadowy fields.

"Don't dig your claws in or you'll hurt her," I said, gripping the bird gently with my knees. I glanced over my shoulder and saw the flamingo's thin pink legs pointing straight out behind us. She was as long and fast as any broom.

"Crazy comets, this is brilliant," I cried as the flamingo shot through the air like a spear. "Every witch should get one!" It was much easier – and far more fun – to ride a fluttering feathery bird than a slippery wooden broomstick.

"There it is," I cried, pointing to the tall white windmill as the flamingo swooped over a line of trees. A swaying lantern hung in the porch, guiding us across the fields like a lighthouse at sea.

Even before we landed, I could see the dark shadow of a jet-black cat, staring up at the sky. "Mum!" called Rascal, leaping off the flamingo's back.

"Careful!" I cried, but his mother didn't even wait for him to land.

"Where've you been, Number Three?" she hissed, cuffing him round the ears with her paw. "I've been worried out of my nine lives."

The flamingo skidded to a stop. I climbed

down and patted her neck. "Thank you for bringing us here!" I whispered, wishing she could understand me in the way Rascal could.

His mother had already stopped hissing. Her anger and worry were gone and she was licking him, purring with love and relief as he explained everything that had happened since he first climbed into the box of old books. "You and your curiosity!" she sighed.

I smiled, happy we had returned him to her so easily. But I was sad too at having to say goodbye. I would miss the brave, inquisitive little kitten.

Just as I was clearing my throat to wish him good luck, his mother turned towards me. Her fiery orange eyes glistened in the darkness. "So my boy's to be a witch's cat now is he?" she purred. "I couldn't be more proud. My own great-grandmother was a witch's companion. Greatest honour any cat can have."

"Oh no, you don't understand," I said quickly, purring politely in my smoothest Cat Chat. "Rascal – I mean Number Three – can't stay with me, Mrs Cat. I was just bringing him home to you and his Person family."

"The family can't keep him. They don't know what is going to happen now their shop has been closed down," said the cat. "They wanted to find him and check he was safe, but he'll need a new home for sure. They've already given Number Two to an old man in the village. They're only keeping Number One because he's big and strong and can catch mice and rats."

"I can catch rats," said Rascal proudly. "There's a huge one behind the dustbins at Hawk Hall. I pounced on it once, but it turned into a puff of black smoke and bit my tail."

"Oh dear," I laughed. "I don't think that's an ordinary rat – it sounds like my grumpy old wand. I told you it ran away."

"Brave boy. You are ready to leave home," said Rascal's mother. "You will make a fine magic cat – I knew your eyes are as green as emeralds for a reason. All witches' cats have green eyes, you know." Her own fiery eyes sparkled. "Go with Miss Bella. Help her with her spells and ride the skies on a broomstick or…" She looked at the flamingo and shook her head in confusion. "Or a big pink bird, at any rate."

"I will." Rascal puffed himself up with pride as Mrs Cat straightened his whiskers. "I'll be the best witch's cat ever."

"But … you can't live with me," I said. I felt as if I was pelting the tiny kitten with stones. "You know I'd love to take you home, more than anything. But the Ables won't let me have a cat."

"Oh!" Rascal made a tiny mewing sound halfway between a sniff and a cough. "Doesn't matter. I'm very busy here anyway," he said. "I have rats and mice to catch..." Then he turned away without another word and hung his head low. I'd never heard him so silent before. I would rather he hissed and scratched at me than this.

"You named him," said his mother. "That means he's bonded to you now."

"I'm sorry." I shook my head. "He'll find a lovely new home again in no time ... he's ... well, he's very cute." I knew that would go to Rascal's head. But it was true; there must be hundreds of Persons who'd want an adorable little kitten like him.

"I have brought you here safely," I said,

blowing Rascal a kiss. "But now I have to find the hope moth and get back to Honeysuckle Cottage."

I took a step towards the windmill. Out of the corner of my eye, I saw Rascal creep forward as if to follow me.

"Shoo!" I hissed, clapping my hands at him, although I felt as if my heart was going to break.

"Come along, Number Three!" His mother stalked off into the darkness.

"My name is Rascal!" he said, arching his back like a lion cub as he followed her into the gloom.

"Yes, it is! You'll always be Rascal to me," I called after him.

But, before I could hear his answer, the door to the windmill swung open and a small child stood yawning in the moonlight. My heart leapt.

I knew her. It was the little girl from the bus – the one whose big sister smiled at me. They had clapped their hands and sung "Wheels on the Bus" together.

"Gretel," I whispered, crouching down so that I was the same height as she was. "Hello."

She was wearing my brown frock and the (very) frilly white apron.

I had found my dress at last.

Chapter Nineteen

I stared as Gretel stood stretching in the doorway. She was rubbing her eyes and yawning. Although it was the middle of the night, she was wearing the full Gretel costume – which was miles too big.

"Did you go to sleep in that?" I smiled. Somehow, the ugly brown dress and the hideous (very) frilly apron didn't look silly on her at all. They looked adorable.

Gretel nodded shyly. "My sister said I

could pretend to be in a real fairy tale."

"Your sister is right," I agreed. Gretel looked exactly as if she had walked out of the pages of a storybook.

"I think she'd like to meet your pretty bird," said Gretel, pointing at the flamingo who was resting her beak on my shoulder. "Shall I go and wake her up?"

"No! Not now," I lurched forward before she could go back inside the windmill. It was going to be hard enough to explain to one tiny sleepy girl what I was doing here at midnight with a giant pink flamingo, let alone her big sister too.

Gretel shrugged. "I saw you flying," she yawned, putting her thumb back in her mouth.

"Did you?" I crouched down, hoping she was so sleepy she might think the whole thing had been a dream by morning. "I came here specially to ask you a question," I explained.

"Is it about the dusty thing?" Gretel asked.

"Dusty thing?" Perhaps I hadn't heard her properly. It was hard to understand what she was saying with her thumb in her mouth.

She stuffed her free hand inside the apron pocket. "Look."

My tummy somersaulted as she pulled out the magic jar. "You've got it!" I grinned. "It isn't broken!" But my heart sank as I peered at the cloudy glass. The moth was as grey as ash and barely moving.

"Darkest dungeons," I gasped. It was as if all the hope was fading inside the jar. Gretel was right. The moth was a dusty thing – dusty, grey and dying. I remembered the bright, shiny creature Aunt Hemlock had captured when it first flew out of the Ables' chimney.

One thing was sure: I must have disappointed the Ables very much if this was all that was left of their shiny hope.

The child they had really wished for must have been very different from me.

My chest felt as if a heavy giant was standing on it in iron boots. When I held out my hand it was shaking. "Please, Gretel," I said. "Can I have the jar back?" Perhaps if I could return the moth to Honeysuckle Cottage where it came from, maybe the hope would start to shine again.

"Hmm." Gretel stretched out her hand. The little jar was almost in my fingers when she suddenly stamped her foot. "No! Poor dusty thing…"

She popped her thumb out of her mouth, unscrewed the lid and shook the jar. "Fly away," she cried.

"Stop!" I tried to catch the frail grey creature as it fluttered free, rising into the moonlit sky like a flake of silver ash above a bonfire.

The flamingo made a desperate grab for

it with her beak, but the moth darted sideways. Free from the jar, it seemed to find new strength.

"Now look what you've done!" I cried.

"Oops! Was I naughty?" Gretel's eyes filled with tears.

"No ... of course not. I'm sorry." I crouched down and took the jar from her fingers. How was she to know that by setting the moth free, the hope it carried would vanish like smoke in the sky? "Go back to bed. This is all just a dream with a pretty pink bird in it," I said. Then I leapt on to the flamingo's back. I had to catch the moth. "In the morning, just remember to tell the little grey kitten

166

that Bella said goodbye."

"The grey kitten..." yawned Gretel. "I
wish he had somewhere nice to live." She
waved sleepily and stepped back inside.

"So do I," I whispered.

The pale moth was already above the
windmill, so there wasn't another moment
to lose. I patted the flamingo's neck and
held out the jar like a butterfly net.

Sweep like wings into the sky
Brush the clouds and fly, fly, fly!

I squeezed my legs against the bird as if I
was riding a winged Pegasus. The flamingo
shot upwards like an arrow.

"There!" I cried as a tiny spark of silver
light glowed in the sky. "I can see the moth!"

The flamingo wobbled. Her left wing
dipped low, almost hitting the big white

sails of the windmill.

"What's the matter?" I asked, wishing for the hundredth time that I could speak Flamingo. But the beautiful pink bird flapped harder, raising her left wing just high enough to rise above the building.

"Well done!" I cheered, but the poor flamingo was still tilting to one side. She turned her head and snapped at her wing, as if trying to peck away an irritating flea.

"Is this better?" I tried as hard as I could to balance my weight the opposite way. Leaning as far as I dared along her right wing, I clung to her feathers with one hand and held the empty jar with the other.

"Missed!" I groaned, scooping at the night sky as the silvery moth fluttered just out of reach. I'd have had more luck gathering star dust in a sieve.

I scooped again…

"Get it!" cried a tiny voice (speaking in fast and fluent Cat Chat). "Let me try. I'll catch it with one paw."

"Rascal!" I gasped as his fluffy grey head appeared amongst the feathers on the flamingo's wing. "What are you doing there? No wonder the poor flamingo can't balance."

"Mum said I belong to you now," purred Rascal, scrambling up in front of me so the flamingo was able to fly straight again at last. "I've come to help. Aren't you going to catch the moth?"

"I'm trying," I snapped as the moth dived past me again. "This would have been a whole lot easier without a hairy ball of fluff hiding under there."

"No need to hiss," said Rascal. "Kittens are good at catching moths. I'll show you…"

"Stop!" I cried, trying desperately to grab him as he sprung towards the fluttering silver light. "You're going to fall."

It was too late. The tips of my fingers brushed the end of Rascal's fluffy tail. But he was already tumbling through the dark sky.

Chapter Twenty

"Rascal!" I cried. The tiny kitten was falling fast.

The flamingo swooped like a heron diving for a fish. I clung on with my knees – one hand held the precious jar and the other grabbed wildly for Rascal as he plunged beneath us.

We were so low, my feet brushed the earth before I caught him.

"Yowl!" he yelped as I grabbed hold of

the fluff on the scruff of his neck and swung him safely back on board.

"Well done, Flamingo!" I cheered as she rose in to the sky. A second slower and the little kitten would have hit the ground for sure. "I'm so sorry I hissed at you, Rascal," I choked, burying my head in his soft fur and hugging him tightly. "I know you were only trying to help."

"Trying?" purred Rascal. "I think I did better than that!"

I looked down and saw he had the fluttering hope moth caught gently between his paws. "Whizzing warlocks, you're brilliant!" I scooped the moth into the jar and twisted the lid on tightly. "Thank you, Rascal! You're the best kitten any young witch could hope for. All we have to do now is get the moth home to Honeysuckle Cottage."

Suddenly, the flamingo lurched sideways as something cold and slimy hit us in the face.

"Ouch!" I cried.

"What was that?" yelped Rascal. But I knew the feeling at once ... like being slapped in the mouth by a big wet fish.

"The Curtain of Invisibility," I said. "It is drawn around the Magic Realm. Quick! Turn around."

The flamingo was amazing. She spun like a spider on a pinhead and shot back over the hills of Person World.

"How can something invisible hurt so much?" said Rascal, straightening his crumpled whiskers with his paw.

"I don't know," I laughed, remembering I had asked the very same question when the Curtain of Invisibility hit me the first time. "Thank goodness we didn't fly right through it." I patted the flamingo's back and shuddered, wondering what would have happened if we had ended up in the Magic Realm. Perhaps we would have been stuck there for ever...

"Everything's going to be all right now isn't it?" yawned Rascal, staggering on to my lap. He curled himself up in a sleepy grey ball. Suddenly, he wasn't a brave panther leaping through the sky to save a hope moth, he was just a very tired kitten ready to go home.

"Once we get the jar back to Honeysuckle Cottage, where the Ables are, the magic will start to work again, I am sure of it." I peered through the glass. The moth seemed to be glowing more brightly already. "I might even manage to convince them they want to adopt an inquisitive kitten too," I said, stroking Rascal's ears.

"Of course they'll want me," he yawned. "I'm adorable." Rascal closed his eyes and began to purr. "The very first thing I'm going to do is catch that big brown rat!"

"My old grumpy wand?" I smiled. "Poor thing. It deserves a bit of peace now it's free."

I had no idea if Aunty Rose and Uncle Martin would ever agree to having a cat, but I had to try. Rascal had been so loyal and brave. Without him, the hope moth would have been lost for sure.

I spotted the warm orange lights of Merrymeet village just ahead. "Hooray for our feathery broomstick, the Fabulous Flying Flamingo!" I cheered. "I promise, I'm going to learn your language so I can thank you properly in your own Beak-Speak as soon as I possibly can."

Perhaps she understood me already, as she turned her head and nibbled my knee.

"We saved the hope moth! All three of us together. We make a pretty magical team!"

I whooped, raising the shimmering jar high in the air as we swooped home over the moonlit rooftops of Merrymeet.

"What's that?" Rascal was suddenly wide awake. He sprung to his feet, wobbling on the flamingo's narrow neck as he arched his back.

"Ark!" squawked the flamingo as his claws dug in.

I peered over her feathery head and saw that not all the lights below us were warm and yellow. Sharp blue flashes pierced the darkness too. A familiar scream like a banshee filled the air

"Police Persons," I shuddered, as their car roared through the dark streets below with the sirens blaring. "Quick! Let's get home as fast as we can." The flamingo soared over Hawk Hall and skidded to a stop behind the bird table at the bottom of the Ables' garden.

"Steady," I whispered. Landing on a flamingo is a lot harder than flying. Her skinny legs wobbled like slippery stilts. I slid off her back and rolled over with a bump, hugging the precious jar to my chest.

"Thundering phantoms! That was a close one," I gasped. There was a puff of pink smoke and the flamingo shot towards the ground like a genie disappearing back inside a bottle.

"Yikes!" Rascal darted underneath a bush. "What's happening?"

"It's all right," I laughed. "She's just turning back into a pen. See?" I picked up the plastic feathery biro from the ground. I was fumbling with the slippery jar in my other hand when I heard somebody calling my name.

"Bella Broomstick! Is that you back there?"

I leapt in the air like a startled frog. The jar slid from my shaking fingers…

Time seemed to stand still.

I watched in horror as the glass hit the edge of the stony path and shattered into a thousand tiny pieces.

Whoosh!

The moth shot into the air like a silver bullet from a gun.

"Wait!" I leapt up, trying to catch it. But I knew it was hopeless. With a last burst of shining light, the tiny speck of magic vanished in the dark sky.

It was over. I had no fast flamingo broomstick ready to jump on to now. This time. the hope moth was gone for good.

Chapter Twenty-One

"Bella Broomstick! Is that you?"

The same angry voice was shouting across the lawn. For a moment I thought it was Aunt Hemlock, it sounded so terrifying and cross. Then I realized it was Aunty Rose. Of course! The magic had faded already. Without a spell on her, she had no reason to be kind and loving to me any more.

"Bella?" she hollered again.

"I'm here," I said, creeping out of the shadows. It was getting light. I glanced over my shoulder and saw Rascal stalking along the edge of the lawn. His tail was twitching as he sniffed the grass.

"Where have you been, young lady?" Aunty Rose was standing outside the front door with her hands on her hips.

"Come here where I can see you," she barked.

I took another step forward into the golden light spilling out over the WELCOME mat in the open doorway.

Uncle Martin burst through the garden gate. "You found her!" he puffed, running up the path towards Aunty Rose.

"I'm sorry," I whispered. I had ruined everything — not only my dreams, but theirs as well. For once, Aunt Hemlock's magic had been something truly wonderful and good (even if she had never meant it to be). Her cunning spell might have been a trick, but the Ables really had seemed happy to have me before the hope moth was lost.

"Sorry? Is that all you've got to say for yourself?" Aunty Rose stormed towards me in her fluffy pink slippers. Tears were streaming down her cheeks. "Sorry isn't good enough!"

"I know," I trembled. She must have found out about the spell. "It was wrong. I…"

"Don't ever disappear like that again!" Aunty Rose flung her arms around my neck. "We were so worried."

"Worried?" I said. "You … you're not cross?"

"You vanished without telling anyone where you'd gone," sighed Aunty Rose, hugging me so tightly that I could barely breathe.

"Typical! Just like my mum," purred Rascal, peeping out from under a bush. "Spitting at me one minute and licking my nose the next."

Slowly, I began to smile. Whatever Aunty Rose did, she certainly wasn't going to lick my nose. But Rascal was right. I remembered how Mrs Cat had arched her back and hissed at her lost kitten when I first brought him home. Really she wasn't angry so much as relieved to know he was safe.

"We're not cross," said Uncle Martin gently. "We were just frightened that something had happened to you."

"Imagine how worried we were when we went into your room," Aunty Rose explained. "I only popped my head in to check you were sleeping soundly. But then your bed was empty … and it was the middle of the night … and…"

"I even called the police," said Uncle Martin as the sirens screeched to a stop on the road outside. "I better go and tell them it was a false alarm."

"So … so they're not going to arrest me?" I said. "You're not going to send me away."

"Arrest you?" laughed Uncle Martin.

"Of course not," said Aunty Rose. "This

is your home, Bella. You belong here."

"But … what about the moth … the magic?" I mumbled. My legs were shaking so much they almost gave way beneath me. Nothing made any sense. Why would the Ables want to keep me now the spell was broken?

"Moth? Magic? Whatever are you talking about?" chuckled Aunty Rose. "There's nothing magic here … just warm hearts and a welcoming home."

"But that *is* magic," I grinned. And at last I understood. The Ables wanted me to stay … and not because Aunt Hemlock had tricked them with a spell.

"You're part of our family, Bella," said Uncle Martin, wrapping a blanket around my shoulders.

There were so many things I wanted to say. My heart was fluttering faster than the hope moth's wings, it was so full with happiness and love. But all I could manage was a sort of gulping sound like a frog. "Thank you!" I croaked. "I'll be the best child you could ever hope for."

Aunty Rose shook her head. "Just be yourself, Bella," she said, firmly. "Warts and all."

"Bursting blisters! Have I finally grown a wart?" I asked, confused.

"No!" laughed Uncle Martin, as I rubbed my nose.

"All I meant is that we're going to get along fine, just the way we are," smiled Aunty Rose.

Galloping galaxies! The Ables liked me the way I was! No magic, no warts, no tricks, no spells ... just plain Bella Broomstick.

Chapter Twenty-Two

All the magic tricks were gone and the Ables still wanted me to stay at Honeysuckle Cottage. I was so happy, I could have danced around the dark garden. But Uncle Martin had finished talking to the police and Aunty Rose was looking stern again.

"There'll be no more wandering off without telling us," she said. "Is that clear? What were you doing out here in the middle of the night anyway?"

"Er…" My brain fizzed and popped like a potion. What could I say? I didn't want to lie. Not after I had caused the Ables so much worry and they had been so kind … not if we really were going to be a proper family. But how could I explain? How could I tell them I had flown through the air on a magic flamingo? How would they feel if they knew they were living with a witch?

"For now," said Uncle Martin, waving to the police as they climbed back into their car, "how about you just tell us the important bits?"

"Well that's easy!" purred Rascal in Cat Chat as he marched into the middle of the lawn. "Start with me."

And so I did.

"I found this kitten and he needs a home," I said. "The family he belongs to can't look after him any more…"

"Wait a minute!" I had barely started my story when Mr Seymour poked his long beaky nose through the railings. What did he want now? My fingers twitched on the end of my pink flamingo pen as I thought of the way that he had treated Gretel's family – closing down their bookshop and throwing them out of their home. I wished I could wave my feathery wand and cast a spell on him right now. That would teach him a lesson.

Three Spells That Would Serve Mr Seymour Right
1: Warts on his big, nosy nose!

2: Turn <u>him</u> into a windmill.

3: Decorate his boring grey concrete with doodles of cute fluffy kittens wearing bow ties (and flamingoes as well).

Or perhaps I should simply turn him into a frog (and Piers too, just for fun!)

But this was the Person World and I had promised myself there would be *NO MORE MAGIC!* I slid the flamingo pen safely behind my ear where it couldn't do any damage. I would just have to hope that there was some other way I could help Gretel and her family.

"Stop!" Mr Seymour was waving his arms and jumping up and down. Piers ran out of the house too, wearing his pyjamas. I was surprised he didn't sleep in his bow tie.

"Don't let those police officers leave before I have had a chance to speak to them," shouted Mr Seymour.

My heart froze. Why did Mr Seymour want to speak to the Police Persons so urgently? Had Piers remembered that I had turned him into a worm? The Police would take me away from the Ables and throw me into gaol after all.

"What can we do for you this time, Mr Seymour?" said the tallest Police Person, climbing slowly back out of the car.

"Spotted any flying carpets? Or alien spaceships?" muttered the shorter one, giggling into his sleeve. "Or a witch on a broomstick perhaps?"

The icy panic in my heart was spreading to my fingertips.

"This may be a joke to you," Mr Seymour sniffed. "But I have called the station three times already. You do not seem to be taking this seriously but I have seen a—"

"Rat!" screamed Piers, as an enormous furry brown creature ran across his yellow velvet slippers.

"Told you, Bella!" screeched Rascal, dashing after it.

There was a flash of brown fur, the swish of a tail and the wink of a black beady eye as the creature leapt through the railing and scuttled under a bush. I recognized my old grumpy wand!

"Thank you!" I whispered in my best Rat Rattle as the leaves rustled and the end of his thick pink tail disappeared.

"I don't think it's us you need. It's pest control," chuckled the tall Police Person.

Mr Seymour was hiding inside one of his empty concrete plant pots. The rat had obviously given him quite a shock. It wasn't as good as a vanishing spell or giant green warts on the end of his nose, but at least someone had managed to teach him a lesson.

Piers was as white as a ghost too as they both shot back inside their big grey house and slammed the front door behind them.

"Dear, oh dear!" The Police Persons were

giggling loudly as they climbed back into their car. Even Aunty Rose was trying not to smile.

But Uncle Martin was frowning. "Rats in the garden? I don't like that," he said peering under the bush where the rat had vanished. "They eat birds' eggs you know."

"What we need," said Aunty Rose, winking at me, "is a cat."

So that is how the four of us – Aunty Rose, Uncle Martin, Rascal and me – stepped over the WELCOME mat together ... and became the family who live at Honeysuckle Cottage.

Before we went to bed, we all sat at the kitchen table and had a warm drink.

"We'll call this little fellow's family first thing in the morning and tell them we have agreed he can stay here," said Uncle Martin, patting Rascal's head as the kitten pounced on the end of his dressing gown cord. "I think he knows better than to bother my birds again."

"He most certainly does!" I said, wagging my finger sternly at Rascal. I should have known a big softy like Uncle Martin would be just as kind to a kitten as he was to any other waifs and strays (like little lost chicks and me!).

"I wonder what Mr Seymour was going to tell the police he saw flying over the village this time?" said Aunty Rose, sipping her warm tea.

A dragon?

A flying horse?

A vampire bat?

"I don't know," Uncle Martin shook his head. "But it's the strangest thing ... I could swear I spotted a pink flamingo in the sky tonight!"

"A flamingo? Round here?" Aunty Rose raised her eyebrows. "Sometimes I think you must have feathers in that big bald egg-head of yours," she giggled.

Rascal and I looked at each other but neither of us said a word (not even in Cat Chat).

"He's only teasing you, Bella," smiled Aunty Rose, "because he knows how much you like that pen of yours."

"I love it!" I said, stroking the soft pink feathers which were tucked safely behind my ear. "It's the most magical thing ever to come out of the Sellwell Department Store!"

"That's good," nodded Uncle Martin. "You can take the pen to school with you when you start next week."

"School?" I gasped.

"Of course," said Aunty Rose. "Don't look so worried. It's all arranged. First thing on Monday morning, we'll go down to Merrymeet Primary and meet the head."

"The head!" I shivered, remembering Dr Rattlebone's bony skull bouncing across the dungeon floor at Creepy Castle.

"You'll make lots of lovely friends," said Aunty Rose. "And you know someone there already."

"Really?" I said, thinking of Gretel's smiley big sister. She looked about the same age as me.

"Piers Seymour will be in your class, for sure," chuckled Uncle Martin.

Piers Seymour? That's all I need.

"Slithering snakes! I'm hopeless at school," I groaned.

But perhaps it would be better in the Person World. And I'll always have Honeysuckle Cottage to come home to.